They Counted Us Out

Willie Craddick Jr.

They Counted Us Out
Willie Craddick Jr.

Printed in the United States of America

First Printing, 2018

ISBN-13: 978-1981841608
ISBN-10: 1981841601

Created and published with Phyl Campbell and the Creative Writing and Publishing Workshop
www.phylcampbell.com

This book is for every teen that struggles with disappointment or depression.

For everyone who has fought the odds — and won!

For everyone that is working towards their dreams.

For everyone who has big dreams and chases them — don't ever stop!

Other books by Willie Craddick Jr:

The Life of a Boy with Big Dreams

Shanae

Shanae adjusted her cap and gown and studied her reflection in the dingy mirror above her bureau. Graduation was still a month away, but Shanae was long past worrying about all that.

She heard her little sister singing in the other room. Before the noise could wake their mother, Shanae slipped the cap and gown off, laid them on the bed, and went to her sister's room. She tapped on the door, didn't wait for an answer -- sister probably wouldn't have heard the tapping over her own singing anyway -- and went into the room with a finger on her lips. The eight-year-old stopped singing. She jumped off the bed and ran to the closet, where she pulled out a top and jeans.

"Forgot. Sorry," Shanae's sister mumbled. She appeared contrite.

"I think we're okay. Thank you," Shanae whispered back. She smiled wide to show she wasn't mad.

Her sister smiled back.

Shanae's mother worked the overnight shift and barely crawled into bed before the sisters had to get ready for school. Her sister's dad wasn't in the picture anymore. Shanae hadn't even met her own dad.

There were some mornings when her sister didn't want to stop singing or playing, and some mornings where it was a fight to get her out of bed. These days often woke their mother, leaving everyone tired and upset. Most of the time, however, her sister cooperated, so Shanae was happy she could help out. She knew some of her friends had siblings that were much more annoying.

Breakfast this morning was a simple event consisting of toast with grape jam and glasses of milk for each sister.

"Can we get cereal next week? Or toaster waffles?" Shanae's sister asked.

"I'll ask Mom," Shanae promised. "It should be okay."

"You say 'okay' a lot, Shanae. How come?"

"Because okay is better than not okay."

"That's silly."

"Well, sometimes I'm silly. And you know what, Sissie?"

"What?"

"Being silly is okay."

"Oh!" Shanae's sister pursued her lips and pointed a scolding finger at Shanae. But when Shanae laughed it off, her little sister laughed, too.

"Finish your milk and brush your teeth. Your bus will be here soon." Shanae returned to her room and hung her cap and gown safely in the closet.

In a month, she would hear the principal call her name.

In a month, she would walk across that stage.

In a month, she would get her diploma and begin her whole new life.

She thought about all the people who had counted her out. She imagined them lined up like class pictures in the yearbook. With a thick black marker, she crossed them out of her life.

"Sissie's bus is here, Momma. And I'm out, too," Shanae called down the hall before she opened the front door and closed it behind herself.

A month from now, she thought, no one would ever count her out again.

Thomas

"That cereal will not taste better for sitting there," Thomas's mother warned. "Hurry up and eat it."

Thomas watched his mother put his sister's lunch in a sack. He lifted the spoon up from the bowl, watching the milk drip from the tip. The date on the carton was two days ago, but his mother insisted it was still fine. It didn't taste fine.

"I'm tired of cereal." Ruby said what they were both thinking. But then she added, "When Daddy gets back, can we have eggs?"

"Sure baby," their mother agreed. Thomas thought his mother would promise Ruby the moon if she thought it would help.

"When is Daddy coming back?" Ruby pressed.

"Soon, baby."

Another lie.

"Now eat your breakfast."

Ruby put a spoonful of cereal into her mouth and made a face. Thomas didn't blame her. Their older brother Jeremy was passed out on the couch in the living room. Thomas remembered when his older brother used to be fun to hang around. But that was a lifetime ago.

"Thomas, can you take Ruby to school today?"

"Yes!" Ruby pumped her fist in the air.

"Sure." Thomas was in no position to argue. He only had a car to drive because Jeremy's license was suspended. That, and the landlord didn't allow cars to stay parked on the street indefinitely. The street was already too narrow in case of an emergency, Thomas had heard explained, but then he didn't believe that, either. It didn't matter what Thomas believed. Cars could only be in front of homes if a licensed driver was inside. Before Thomas was old enough to drive, they tried to sell the car to help pay some of Jeremy's legal bills. But there were no decent offers. Then their dad got laid off.

And maybe Thomas hadn't helped things. He'd wanted a new ten-speed bike. And he should have gotten it. After all, Jeremy got to claim the entire living room as his room while Thomas went to sharing his room with Ruby. The baby, and a girl. How else was he supposed to see her? The least his parents could have done was buy him a bike to get around. With a bike, a good bike, he could deliver newspapers or run errands for people. A bike didn't need gasoline or expensive repairs -- just some air for the tires every now and then. He got so big for his old bike that when he pedaled, his knees hit his ears.

He tried to ask nicely, and to be patient. He tried to explain that if he had a good paper route, he could help pay bills and a good bike was an investment into his future. It didn't matter. No one listened to the middle kid, anyway.

Then, last year, their dad woke him up in the middle of the night and said he had to see about a job. He was gone for three days. Everyone wanted to know what happened, but Thomas was so sure he'd dreamed it that he didn't tell anybody. When their dad returned, he said he'd told Thomas where he was, which he didn't, and as if that explained everything, which it didn't. It might have explained, if the job had worked out, if that was even the truth, but it didn't and it didn't solve anything. Thomas got up and put his cereal bowl in the sink. It was still half-full, but the souring milk clung to the roof of his mouth and he just couldn't stomach another swallow.

"Thomas, that's so wasteful. I paid good money for that food!"

Another lie, he thought. "Sorry, Ma." Another lie.

"I don't know what you think I'm going to do," his mother was saying. Thomas had heard it before. He just couldn't listen again.

Another night, about six weeks after his dad left the first time, his dad left again. And so far, he hadn't returned. Thomas knew his father didn't say anything to him that second time. But everyone else thought he must have, and Thomas just wasn't saying. That was months ago. And still, eight-year-old Ruby clung to the hope that Daddy was coming back.

Thomas's old bike was now hers. She'd wrapped it in ribbons and stickers and tied pink streamers to the handles. No self-respecting boy could ride it anymore. He knew a lot of his classmates would be thrilled to have a car. At this point, he would trade the car and either his sister or his brother or both to any one of them just to have his own room – and a bike wouldn't hurt.

Thomas was never going to have kids. He was going to have dogs. Dogs didn't care what you smelled like or how much money you had. And the job he got walking dogs was also thanks to responsibility that Jeremy had abandoned. He didn't really want to walk other people's dogs. He wanted a dog to call his own. But that wasn't going to happen. Even Ruby stopped pleading for a dog months ago. Not long after Dad left. At least Ruby was the only one who didn't hold Dad's absence against him. For now.

So Thomas was blamed for a lot of things that had very little to do with him. And he took on a lot of responsibility for crap other people neglected. Would it kill anyone to hand him an easy button for ONCE?

"C'mon Ruby." He called over his shoulder to his sister. "Your chariot awaits."

J'Shawn

J'Shawn waited for the bailiff to call his name. It was all a big misunderstanding. He had never been in trouble before. That damn cheat out at the mall. This was all her fault, really.

When it was his turn, J'Shawn said, "I paid for Beats, Your Honor." He tried to remember all the things he was supposed to. Be respectful. Look at her, but not look at her defiantly. Don't fiddle with his clothes. Hands at his sides. "But what was in my box wasn't Beats. At first, I didn't notice anything wrong and I was just excited to have something that would play my tunes. I worked really hard to afford the Beats, Your Honor."

The woman behind the bench was a greying black woman who reminded J'Shawn of his Auntie MayBelle. She was his grandmother's sister. She was really good at cards and kept the best candy in her purse. She acted all stern when her sister was in the room, but she dropped the act when her sister went to the kitchen or the bathroom or to speak to the orderlies that managed Auntie's care at the home. He asked once why Auntie didn't just live with her sister, like most folks did, but Auntie just laughed and said she liked her lifestyle and that her sister would cramp it. J'Shawn wasn't sure what she'd meant by that.

"So what was the problem, young man?" the judge prompted.

"Well, Your Honor, the headphones crapped out in less than a week, and I took them back to the store."

"You're charged with shoplifting," the judge leaned forward. "How do you plead?"

J'Shawn thought she hadn't said it in an angry way, but he also figured he needed to get to the point and not try her patience.

"Yes, ma'am. Your Honor," J'Shawn corrected. "When I took the headphones that I'd bought to the clerk with my receipt, she put both of them behind the counter and told me to leave."

The judge squinted her eyes a little, like she wasn't sure she heard correctly. "Go on."

J'Shawn took a deep breath. "I'm not proud of what I did next, but she had the headphones and the receipt. So I told her I was going to make an exchange whether she liked it or not. Then I grabbed the nearest box of Beats off the shelf and left the store."

The judge frowned. "Why didn't you ask to speak to a manager?"

"She's the only one we ever saw in that store, Your Honor."

"We?"

"Me and my friends. And it was my word against hers, and she kept my receipt."

"Did you make a copy of it?"

"No, ma'am."

"I see. What about a bank statement or some other proof that you made that purchase?"

"I paid cash ma'am. Your Honor. All the proof I had was that receipt."

"That is a problem, young man. I agree," the judge said thoughtfully. "There were certainly other ways to handle this situation."

"Yes, Your Honor."

"But I do believe you."

J'Shawn looked at the judge with renewed hope.

"I see here you're a senior at East End."

"Yes, Your Honor."

"Are you a good student there?"

"I'm on the honor roll, Your Honor. B average. And I've never had a referral."

"I believe that, too. Do you know that East End is my Alma Mater as well?"

"No, Your Honor. I didn't know that."

"So here's what I'm going to do," the judge said. "I can't just dismiss the charges. You admit you stole the headphones, no matter what the circumstances. But instead of a jail time or even community service and a record, I'm going to put you on probation until the day you graduate. That means no DWIs, no speeding tickets, no drug use, and absolutely no shoplifting. If you can do that, and stay out of trouble, this incident won't go on your permanent record. You'll avoid a trial and I'll even write you a letter of recommendation for college."

"Thank you, Your Honor."

"Have you applied for college?"

"I have a football scholarship, but I'll lose it if this goes on my permanent record."

"Then you have an even larger incentive to make sure that doesn't happen."

"Yes, ma'am. Your Honor."

"Hey, us East Enders have to stick together." The judge smiled at J'Shawn before making a last note in the file and handing it to the bailiff. "See the clerk on your way out. Bailiff, next case, please."

J'Shawn walked out of the courtroom in a daze. He stumbled to the clerk's window. There, he learned that the judge had waived his court costs. And she wasn't making him pay for the stolen Beats. The clerk handed him an excuse for school and J'Shawn walked outside.

The sun was warm on his face despite winter's lingering chill. He drove his car to the gas station, parked next to the pump, and turned off the engine. The needle on his gas gauge had been hovering around the E for three days. If he'd had to pay fines and court costs, he'd have had to sell the car and walk to school and work. Instead, he was going to be OK. He was going to be OK.

L'Monica

"Settle down, people. Settle down."

L'Monica glanced around the classroom discreetly as the seniors took their seats and came to order. Ms. Mathis was a nice teacher, and her classroom felt homey, not quite so much like an empty gallery they forgot to fill with art. But Ms. Mathis also didn't play. Maybe she was fifty? L'Monica had never been good at telling adults' ages. She'd been the business teacher long enough that several BETA club trophies in the school display had her name on them as sponsor.

"BETA Nationals are in two weeks, and I want to make sure all of you are ready to compete. What's the first thing you need, class?"

"A product!"

"And second thing?"

"A business plan!"

"And finally?"

"A smile!"

"Very good." Ms. Mathis smiled warmly.

L'Monica couldn't help but smile back. The students who would be representing the school in the main competition had been ready for weeks.

Her friend Ebony had a store, Bling Thing, with cell phone covers and accessories. It was very popular and most of the students at school had one of Ebony's phone fashion statements. Some of the teachers and staff did, too.

Another girl, Shanae, had a reading app for kids. L'Monica wanted to know more about it, but she didn't have siblings or reading problems, so asking seemed weird.

Then there was the boy in the back who created music for people. Miss Mathis called him the B2B leader because he made music tracks for his classmate's businesses or activities. He didn't do many sales for the student body at large.

Last year's national winner actually sat two seats diagonal from her. Jason had red-tipped black hair and stood over six foot tall. He could sell diet pills to starving people. L'Monica had seen him last summer at Farmer's Market selling the apron he was wearing to this middle-aged white woman when he ran out of T-shirts. The woman paid top dollar and had him sign it. It was amazing.

As if he could feel her looking, Jason turned around then and caught her eye. He smiled at her briefly before turning his attention back to Ms. Mathis. It wasn't a pervy smile, or even an interested one. Jason was friendly, but he was all business.

L'Monica's own business venture was good, but she wasn't the salesman Jason was, at least not yet. She was good with photography and she liked to take pictures. After her grandma died, she created a photo montage that they played during the funeral. She got lots of compliments on it. When asked to create a business, L'Monica created Rosemary, offering photo montages for senior pictures, special events, pet owners, and, of course, memorials. She was only a sophomore, but Rosemary was successful enough to allow her to join the senior BETA group. Miss Mathis had told her she had a spot as an alternate for Nationals, but she figured the only way she would actually get to go was if one of the seniors actually needed her memorial services.

At the front of the room, Ms. Mathis gave a few more instructions, then pronounced "back to work!" and most of the seniors headed to the adjoining computer lab to finish presentations.

J'Shawn came in and handed Ms. Mathis an excuse slip. What was he wearing a tie for? L'Monica wondered.

"How did it go?" Ms. Mathis asked gently.

"Probation. From now until graduation."

"They didn't throw the case out?" Jason asked incredulously.

"Nah, I did it. It's fine."

"They should close that lady down for cheating us. You know you weren't the only one."

"Man, it's cool. Just be cool."

"Well, you're lucky it was just probation," Ms. Mathis said.

"Yes, ma'am," J'Shawn agreed.

"Though from what I've heard from several students, that store can't remain in business indefinitely. And I'd trust you and Jason long before someone selling knock-off electronics to anyone."

"Thank you, Ms. Mathis."

So that's what it was. Several of L'Monica's classmates had legal issues that needed to be dealt with.

"Ms. Mathis, I can't get my presentation to load."

"I'm coming, Shanae."

The productive buzz of the room made this class L'Monica's hands-down favorite. She'd prefer working outside, taking pictures. But on days she needed to be editing and compiling in the studio, if it had energy like this, it would be bearable.

She looked down at her worksheet. "What is the story behind your business name?"

L'Monica's pencil hovered over the worksheet. She couldn't just write, "Grandma," though that was true enough. Ebony had suggested she talk about Ophelia and Hamlet, since all the seniors read it and knew about the flowers –- specifically Rosemary for remembrance -- mentioned in Ophelia's mad scene. But Rosemary was just her grandmother's name. And that was enough. Didn't need to bring Shakespeare into it.

At the same time, did she want a bunch of strangers asking her about her grandma all the time?

Maybe it would be better to say it was from the play. It would make a good sales story, as Ms. Mathis called it, especially by the time she was a senior and has actually studied Hamlet. But was that a betrayal, somehow, to her grandmother's memory? L'Monica didn't know.

***

They sat down to lunch together. Ebony was grilling J'Shawn about his court appearance. Shanae was talking to Jason about his presentation. L'Monica was just taking it all in. She wished she had her camera. She liked the way her classmates came in twos and threes, before they sat down at the round tables with the attached stools. Ebony stood tall as she could with her books clutched to her chest. J'Shawn stood with one foot on a stool, his books on the table just to the side of his spot. Jason always sat quickly with his lunch. L'Monica wondered if that was because he was so tall. In fact, sitting down to eat, he was still just a little below Ebony's eye level. The other BETAs filled in around them. She knew their names, but she didn't pay them much attention. They weren't her competition like Jason and Shanae were. She turned her focus back to them.

Jason was telling Shanae about the photo shoot he was planning for his clothing line. He was setting it up for the weekend before Nationals. L'Monica wished he would have asked her. But probably he put it into his budget, and a professional photographer probably looked more legit than another student.

But now there were too many people around and L'Monica couldn't isolate the conversation.

A boy named Thomas took the empty seat next to her. "Hi. You gonna eat that?"

L'Monica turned the apple over in her hands. "Eventually."

"That's cool," Thomas said. He plunged his spoon into the rice and sauce mixture that was on his tray.

L'Monica wrinkled her nose.

Ebony finished her conversation and took her place on the other side of L'Monica. "One day, I'm going to marry that man," she sighed.

"J'Shawn?"

"No." Ebony scoffed. "Jason."

L'Monica couldn't help it. She giggled. "And does Jason know about his upcoming nuptials?"

"Nah. I thought I'd surprise him."

"I don't think that's possible. That boy has his eyes on the prize," L'Monica said.

"Oh, I know," Ebony agreed. "He has no interest in me. That's what makes him so attractive. He's going to be rich, you know."

"Probably. He deserves to be."

"Nobody deserves to be rich," Thomas jumped into their conversation.

"Jason does. And this was a conversation to which you were not invited, boy," Ebony bit off the last word, unblinking eyes on the offending classmate who dared disagree with her.

"Thomas didn't mean it like that," L'Monica wasn't sure why she was defending him, but she felt Thomas's statement was probably more honest than rude.

"I'm just saying, rich is for those who are lucky. Usually those who are born into it. And nobody deserves it. Just like nobody deserves to be in poverty. But it happens."

L'Monica facepalmed. Only the tragically stupid argued with Ebony. She was about as hard-headed as they came.

"Haters gonna hate. Privilege is going to justify. But me and mine, we will rise and rise. Hater."

Thomas started to open his mouth to say something else, but L'Monica cut him off. "Please. I'm just here to eat my apple. Not play referee. Ebony is my friend, so you can sit there and eat your rice or you can kick rocks. Your choice."

"I'm done anyway." Thomas got up from the table.

Ebony stared daggers at him as he took his empty tray to the window. She continued to stare until Thomas found a new table to sit at, at the opposite end of the room. Then she turned back to L'Monica.

"Well done, girlfriend. I knew you couldn't stay shy for long."

L'Monica blushed. She didn't know what to say.

"And I'm very glad you think of me as a friend," Ebony continued. "You do a good job keeping your thoughts to yourself or letting your pictures be a thousand words and all that. But I knew deep down you'd find your voice when you needed to."

"Thanks," L'Monica mustered. She felt a little bit bad for Thomas, sitting by himself. But he pretty much brought it on himself. She continued to palm her apple. She just wasn't hungry.

"Hey," Ebony said. "Are you gonna eat that?"

Thomas

Thomas took a seat at the opposite end of the cafeteria from Ebony, L'Monica, and the other BETAs. He was not a hater. He was just keeping it real. Why did Ebony always have to label anyone she disagreed with as a hater?

But forget them anyway. Thomas' business was a dog walking service. He had inherited, for lack of a better word, the business from his older brother. Part of him worried that Jeremy would snap out of it one day and demand his job back. The car he would give back. But he liked the dogs.

Dogs were much better companions than people. They didn't talk back, and you got used to the butt sniffing. Thomas also found that the owners of the dogs he walked tended to be busy business people, which meant they felt bad they were working all the time and gave Thomas a little more to assuage their guilt. Not enough to actually help Thomas get ahead, but enough that he could afford the gas to drive back and forth to school and to the fancy neighborhood where people actually had lawns and sidewalks and driveways to park in. And money and dogs and guilt.

Thomas was bitter because lots of people needed their dogs walked, but he wasn't immediately hired by all of them. He'd pick up a new client and a reliable one would move away. He didn't want to put money into advertising or expansion in case he started making so much that his brother took it back. Although it would be nice if there was enough work for both of them. Maybe that would help Jeremy. But Jeremy didn't want to be helped. He just wanted to take. Well, Thomas didn't want to have anything he cared about taken.

Then, there was the matter of his classmates and their projects. He liked L'Monica's project because she took really good pictures. He even recommended her to some of the people whose dogs he walked. But as far as he knew, she didn't tell anyone that he walked dogs. It was pretty unfair. However, she was really shy.

Thomas wanted to talk to her about it, but he was nervous around her. He wasn't even sure if he liked her liked her, but he wasn't sure if he didn't. He was sure he didn't like Ebony.

He thought about his problem some more. He needed more clients to show an expansion of his business over the school year. Ms. Mathis didn't feel like his business fit what she wanted, because it didn't have a product. But surely a dog walking service was better than clothes and cell phone accessories. Jason didn't even sew his own clothes. He just added designs and stuff. And he was starting to become popular enough that he could even pay a company to do that.

Ebony was just sticking paint and stickers on cell phone cases and junk. Anyone could do that. Heck, he'd done something similar for a minute. Ebony had actually tried to shut him down. Thomas won that battle, but he lost the war. Everyone in the class sided with Ebony even though Ms. Mathis ruled that he was right.

It served Ebony right when Thomas cut a picture of her head out of the yearbook and pasted it on a picture of a dog he cut out of a magazine in the library. He dropped some sequins onto the picture and captioned it "Bitchin' Bling." It went viral in a day at school, but then people claimed they never liked it and Thomas had to apologize. He lost two dog clients that week and no one bought a single collar from him. He didn't care much. Funny was still funny.

J'Shawn was all about music, which Thomas thought could be useful, but Thomas didn't want to get too close to him. Legal troubles were hanging over J'Shawn's head, and Thomas didn't want to get too close to that. He knew what that road looked like from Jeremy, and if J'Shawn was going down that road too, Thomas was not riding shotgun. On the other hand, maybe Thomas should try to reach out to J'Shawn. Some kind of olive branch to get J'Shawn on his side. Nothing he couldn't live without, of course, but if he could think of a way to add music and support J'Shawn, then maybe J'Shawn would return the favor. After all, who didn't like music?

Shanae was building some sort of app for her little sister. Her sister and Ruby and Jason's little sister were all the same age and sometimes played together at recess or wherever. This was another reason Thomas expected Jason and Shanae to be good to him. But they had their own things going, and no time for anyone but themselves.

L'Monica, though. She had something good going on. Her photography skills were a service, but the montages were a digital product. And she could put them on flash drives or burn CDs. Ms. Mathis was even talking to her about expanding into the memory book business.

But that wasn't helping him. He couldn't try the collars again. That was a disaster. He thought about taking dog food and putting it into smaller containers. He knew his clients hated lugging twenty-pound bags from Tagmart around. But his clients' dogs all ate different brands. So he'd have to spend a lot of money up front to make any money off the idea. And he didn't have that kind of scratch.

The bell rang, and Thomas got up again and made his way to his next class. Other than the potential J'Shawn olive branch, he was just as clueless to help himself with his business project as he was when he first sat down next to L'Monica.

Jacob

"If I had been in the principal's office half as often as you kids, I never would have amounted to anything!"

Jacob told himself not to take the bait. He knew what it looked like, him sitting on the bench waiting for Principal Bellamy to call him in. And he wasn't sure why the principal even called him in the first place. He alternately crumpled and smoothed the excuse slip in his hands.

The physics teacher stood over him menacingly. Wire-rimmed glasses were shoved up and into the man's face. A pocket protector filled with pens filled the too-tight white shirt's breast pocket. The teacher ran one hand through his dark greasy hair and squinted down at Jacob. "If I didn't have to deal with hooligans like you, my job would be exponentially easier!"

"If you didn't have any students, you wouldn't have a job, sir," Jacob said before he could stop himself.

"You're never going to amount to anything with an attitude like that!"

"Sir, you don't even know me," Jacob said.

"I know enough!" The teacher did not back down. "I see where you are sitting and I know where this road leads you. It's the same thing year after year after..."

The door to the principal's office opened before the teacher could finish, but it didn't matter. Jacob had heard it all before. He just wanted to find out whatever it was Principal Bellamy wanted so he could get on with his day.

"Come in, Jacob, please." Principal Miranda Bellamy wore fancy jeans and a school T-shirt. Her curly hair hung in loose waves about her shoulders. She had funky red glasses that she was constantly losing on top of her head. She smiled warmly -- first at Jacob, then at the physics teacher. "You, too, Mr. Avery. Come in, come in. Thanks for making time for me."

Jacob and Mr. Avery filed into the principal's office. Her desk was piled a foot high in manila file folders, but she had a small circular table that only had a few sheets of paper on it and a couple elephant sculptures. The elephant motif continued up the bookcase and was carried out in posters and one cloth hanging -- Jacob forgot what those things were called.

"Please, sit. Mr. Avery, would you get the door behind you, please? Thank you." Principal Bellamy patted her head until she found her glasses. She lifted them off her head and examined the lenses before putting them toward the edge of her nose. At the same time, she made her way around Jacob and the table to sit in front of the piece of paper.

Door shut, Mr. Avery took the only remaining chair so that he and Jacob both faced the principal.

Jacob wished he wasn't sitting so close to the physics teacher, but he couldn't move without creating a scene, and he was very curious to know why the three of them were sitting around the table, anyway.

"I'm sure you're both wondering why I called you in here," the principal said, as if she could read Jacob's mind.

Jacob could tell Mr. Avery was just as confused as he was. Neither of them said anything.

"Well," Principal Bellamy continued brightly, "I just got the results back from the state exams. One of our students earned a perfect score in the science section. I was hoping, Mr. Avery, that you would consider allowing him to join your college prep class..."

"Well, of course! I'm always happy to help another nerd," Mr. Avery agreed.

Impossible, Jacob thought.

"... and Science Bowl. Jacob definitely needs to join Science Bowl."

"Great!" Mr. Avery said enthusiastically.

A bit too enthusiastically, Jacob thought.

"When do I get to meet Jacob? Introduce him to the team?"

Jacob could not believe that the principal winked at him. He stifled a laugh that was building up in his chest. A perfect score on the science section. Not bad. He'd been wondering about that one question about recessive traits in mice under extreme conditions. Guess he answered it right after all. Anyway, it was the English section he struggled with.

As long as the person he was talking to could understand him, why did he need to sound like some stuck up old white dude? He could study English all day every day for a year and never sound like Mr. Avery. Mr. Avery -- who was grinning like an idiot and still hadn't figured out the punchline of the principal's private joke.

"Mr. Avery, meet Jacob. Jacob, I'm sure you already know who Mr. Avery is."

"Yes, ma'am. We've met."

The physics teacher's smile finally came unglued from his face as he took in the complete situation. "This student made the perfect score?"

"Just in science," the principal confirmed. But Jacob isn't just a good test-taker. Last year's science fair project was a knock-out, too."

"I shook hands with all the winners. I would have remembered this one!"

Jacob remembered that day. He was so excited to be presenting at the Science Fair with a great project that he ignored his body and struggled down the stairs to the breakfast table. And his grandmother marched him right back up the stairs and into bed. But she'd brought him soup, and they'd been able to watch Amber's live videos on his tablet. His project had already been set up at school and Amber answered any questions that were asked, going above and beyond the duties of a girlfriend.

"Jacob's girlfriend Amber accepted the award on his behalf due to illness last year, if I recall correctly."

Jacob nodded. That was before she moved away.

"And the award was for genetics, not physics, so you probably didn't give it another thought."

Counting us out all the time, Jacob thought. But he didn't say it. He was, however, enjoying watching Mr. Avery squirm. Maybe a little too much.

"Yes, Mr. Avery. Jacob here has a brilliant mind for science. And I know with your guidance, he is going to be top notch in his field, whatever that may be."

Bio-engineering at UGA, Jacob thought. Youngest geneticist in a decade. He didn't care much for oscillating springs or the terminal velocity of a speeding bus, but after years of being asked if his blue eyes were fake, he had developed an interest in genetics that just couldn't be satisfied. Each year since he was old enough to look stuff up online, he had tackled a different aspect of his own genetic code for the Science Fair. But last year was the first year there were actual judges and not just a participation ribbon. Each year, he realized he was only scratching the surface of discoveries to be made.

He realized Mr. Avery and the principal were both looking at him expectantly. Shoot. "Uh," he started. What had been the last thing someone said? "I hope so?" He said hesitantly, hoping that his words somehow made sense for the conversation.

"Jacob is a young person of few words, Mr. Avery. But I've had my eye on him since he was in middle school. We could be looking at a real live Doogie Howser or Dr. House!"

Mr. Avery put out his hand.

After a moment, Jacob reached out and shook it.

"I guess I owe you an apology, Jacob. And I didn't like it when you said it, but you probably will make more money than a teacher like me."

"It's OK, Mr. A," Jacob said. If Mr. Avery could admit his own error in judgment, then maybe he wouldn't be so bad after all.

"Mr. A. Hmmm. I like that," Mr. Avery said. He released the handshake and patted his pocket protector. "Now, first thing we need to do is."

"Well, actually, Jacob needs to return to class if it's all the same," the principal stood, and motioned for the door. "And I don't need to take up any more of your valuable time. Thanks for stopping in."

"Sure, sure," Mr. Avery said.

"Ok, bye," said Jacob. He should have asked whether to return to class or if it was time for lunch. He was barely aware of his own body as he left the office and entered the hallway.

Mr. Avery kept up both ends of the conversation in his excitement to either make amends or invite a new nerd to the round table.

"Oh, Jacob, I forgot to sign your note," the principal called.

Grateful for a direction, Jacob headed back to the office and met the principal at the door.

She dropped her voice conspiratorially. "You're going to have to be patient with Mr. Avery. He's brilliant, but he's not used to brilliant people looking like us. He's a good teacher and a good man. And you can help get more students involved in areas that, well, they haven't been interested in before." She pulled a pen from behind her ear, flattened the note against the wall, and signed it with a flourish. "Back to third period, you go."

L'Monica

"You already agreed to do it for one fifty! And I don't have another hundred dollars to give you!"

L'Monica heard Jason's voice. He sounded upset. Her hands rested upon the door, unsure whether to open it or give Jason his privacy. But he must have heard the door squeak, because he turned around and caught her eye through the classroom door window and waved her in. He was on the phone.

"Look, I came to you to do business. You've got my deposit. And we agreed I was going to pay the balance the day of the shoot."

L'Monica set her stuff down. She noticed Jason tapping his foot impatiently as he listened to the other end of the conversation. L'Monica partly wanted to hear it, too, and partly wanted to be anywhere else.

"You agreed to give me the discount if I could be flexible on days," Jason continued. "But you have bumped me three times and it's difficult to get my models when they are all not working or studying or previously committed." Jason took in a breath.

L'Monica realized she'd been holding hers.

"You know most of us do our homecoming and prom pictures through your company, right? It would be terrible if we all decided to go with your competitor this year, right?"

Jason listened patiently for the response.

"That's right. East Enders forever. Thank you so much. Have a great day."

He hit a button on his phone and disconnected the call. "He's going to screw me," he said.

"Well, it sounded like he was listening," L'Monica offered.

"I was grateful he gave me the discount." Jason half sat, half leaned against the table. "But he's holding it over my head. Now it's costing me in other ways. I would just ask for my deposit back, but me finding another photographer now doesn't mean I won't get the same run around."

L'Monica wanted to say he wouldn't get the same run around from her. She wanted to remind him about the work she did and how much people liked it.

But she didn't want to seem braggy when he was genuinely upset.

Jason didn't know how to read her silence, and so he took it as judgy. "I have to hustle, OK?"

L'Monica wasn't sure if Jason was actually talking to her or just venting out loud. "Excuse me?" "People think I won this thing and I'm all that, but what y'all don't realize is that there are all these strings attached. And they won't stretch like I need them to."

L'Monica hadn't realized. She thought he, of all people, had it made.

"The first time I won that trophy? One of my friends tried to swipe it. Thought it was real gold they could trade in for drugs or something. They ain't my friend no more, and that's not the point."

Tried to steal Jason's trophy? What a crappy friend. And besides, anyone who touched one of the trophies or even looked at it close knew that it was basically painted plastic. The base was probably worth more than the award on top. L'Monica didn't let her eyes leave Jason's.

"And all those prizes that I won? Really just like coupons. I'm working three jobs to pay for a photoshoot that I supposedly won. Because it's an investment into my future."

"Damn," L'Monica replied softly. A little louder, she asked, "But can't your folks help out?"

"No." Jason shut her down instantly. "And I don't want to talk about them anyways."

L'Monica stepped back. She'd never seen Jason so angry and upset. Here she thought he had it made. "So if there's no point to any of this, why are you still killing yourself to make it?"

"Because they counted me out."

Jason's voice went deadly calm, with a determination that L'Monica recognized. It was certainly attractive. There was this quiet power and control in his voice that she could appreciate.

"Who did?" She whispered. Everyone L'Monica knew voted Jason Most Likely to Succeed. And why shouldn't they?

"Everybody. Everybody who expected me to fail. Everybody who just wanted me to succeed so they could get their cut. Everybody who used me as a bargaining chip for whatever game they thought they were playing."

L'Monica watched Jason count off on his fingers.

"But I'm gonna get out of here for a while. Try Hollywood or maybe New York City. Hustle hard and make something of myself. And if I'm lucky. It's not if, though. Not really. Teacher's always saying that line from that movie, 'luck favors the prepared,' you know? Well, I'm getting as prepared as I can."

The late bell rang.

"I gotta catch the bus so I can get to work. See you tomorrow?"

"Yeah, sure. See you."

***

L'Monica was still thinking about their conversation as she helped her mother cook dinner later that evening.

"Mama?"

"Hmmm?" Her mother gave the sauce a stir, then set more vegetables on the block for her to chop.

"I was talking to Jason today. You know that one guy that won all the awards and stuff?"

Her mother wiped her hands on her apron, then checked the bread in the oven before answering. "Now L'Monica, don't you be trying to butter me up. You know you aren't dating until you are 18 and that's final."

"No, Momma. Not like that. We were just talking." L'Monica finished the carrots and started on the celery.

"Good. So about what were the two of you 'just talking,' hmmm?"

"Well, I thought he won and his life was all set. And that's not the way. Lots of girls want to date him. Ebony is already planning her wedding to him. But it's almost like winning may have put a target on his back, you know?"

"He is not moving in here." Her mother swiped the chopped carrots into a bowl, but she stopped to look L'Monica in the face.

"No, Mamma." That thought hadn't even crossed L'Monica's mind, actually. Where would her mother think another person would fit? Their apartment was barely big enough for the two of them. "But his talking just got me thinking about what I want. Or maybe what I don't want."

"What do you mean, baby?"

L'Monica noticed how her mother held the bowl in front of her. Her mother's knuckles went pale with the strain of not dropping the bowl -- which had nothing to do with the weight of the bowl or the carrots inside. L'Monica didn't quite understand why her mother seemed so tense. She fought to find the words to express herself and get her mother to relax. Pictures were easier. "When Grandma died, and we had her funeral and I did the pictures, it really helped. And it helped other people."

"A picture's worth a thousand words, that's the truth."

"And when I take pictures for people, they're usually so happy. Even if they were having a bad day. I just listen, and shoot, and they pose and talk. By the end of a session, they're not fixed, but they seem better." L'Monica went back to chopping celery, grateful to have something to do with her hands.

"You're a good listener, L'Monica. People warm up to you quick." She dumped the bowl of carrots into the sauce and retrieved a head of lettuce from the fridge.

"And that's enough for me, I think." L'Monica spoke hesitantly.

"You're still going to college, young lady."

"Yeah, but I don't have to go to the fanciest school for some expensive degree. I can go local, learn more about being an entrepreneur with a business degree, and hopefully graduate without being in debt. I'm pretty sure my grades are good enough for merit scholarships, and then you won't have to work so hard or worry so much." The more L'Monica spoke, the more confident she felt.

"I'm your mother. Worrying about you IS my job more than my job at the dentist's office is." She reached out for the knife.

Done with chopping, L'Monica handed it over. "I know. And I know why you're so strict with me. I know I'm lucky to have a mom like you."

"What do you want?" L'Monica's mother stopped with the knife in midair.

L'Monica giggled. "Really nothing, Momma. I just love you, that's all."

"MmmmHmm!"

Ebony

Ebony thought up The Bling Thing after she'd broken her screen for the third time and the phone store said insurance wouldn't replace it anymore. Her boyfriend had bought her first phone, and a case. And to mark his territory, he had written their names on the phone case in permanent marker. In a heart. Ebony had thought it was sweet. Until she saw another girl's phone case with her boyfriend's name on it in a very similar heart. She took her phone out of its case and left the case for him to find. And then she took him back. Again and again.

J'Shawn and Jason warned her that her king was nothing but a joker, but Ebony was stubborn. And she wanted someone to love her. But she couldn't keep paying the deductible to repair the screen and she couldn't afford a new phone, and she wasn't the artist her boyfriend was. But she marked over the name-filled heart on her phone and then tried to color over the entire case. The result was awful. She tried several different markers, paints, even nail polish. Some things worked better than others. Some paints applied well, but they couldn't handle being twisted or bent when the case was taken off the phone. Paints cracked and flaked, marker sweat off in her hand. One thing after another was one disaster after another. Still, she persisted.

At the dollar store, she'd found bling stickers beside the nail polish. At two for a buck, she figured what the heck, and bought some to apply to her ruined phone cover.

And it was far from perfect, but it was a start. The Joker, as her friends now referred to him, was back in her life. So the stickers came off and the paint came off until the heart was once again visible. And then he cheated again, and the nail polish and stickers came back out. Ebony spent a lot of time making her trashed case look better than she felt inside. And one day, it looked pretty good. Shanae even told her it did. It felt good to be doing something with her hands, even if it was just something for her. She went back to the dollar store and got more stickers. Then she passed a bin of covers that were on clearance. An idea began to form in her mind.

She didn't have a lot of spending money, but she used what she had to buy clearance-priced cases, and more bling. The next day at school, she sold the tricked out cases. She used the money to buy more cases, glad that no one else had bought out the dollar store while she was at school. One thing led to another, and The Bling Thing was born.

Jason told Ms. Mathis about what Ebony had done, so Ms. Mathis called her out of her regular class to talk to her. Ebony was afraid she would get in trouble for selling things at school, but Ms. Mathis appreciated the entrepreneurial spirit Ebony had. She invited Ebony to switch into her marketing class with Jason and J'Shawn. Ebony didn't need to be asked twice.

J'Shawn

"What?" J'Shawn pulled his headphones off his head. He did not turn around to see who was behind him. He didn't even hang the headphones around his neck. He kept his hands on the earpieces just slightly above his head, indicating that whoever was bothering him should make it quick.

"Make a playlist for me for when I'm walking the dogs," Thomas was saying.

Every day was a work day in the marketing classroom. J'Shawn had been listening to some tracks he had recorded from the night before. They were pretty dope, but there was something about the bass line that was wasn't quite right.

"Fifty dollars," J'Shawn said, put his headphones back on, and turned back around. Thomas didn't even say "please."

And he never had any money. He bummed everything -- ideas, clothes, shoes. J'Shawn did not know what Ms. Mathis saw in him. Maybe she just pitied him?

But J'Shawn did not work for free.

"Come on!" Thomas begged in an unattractive way. "I'll tell the people whose dogs I'm walking who put my playlist together and I'll tell you which songs the dogs like. Hey! I've got an idea! You could do a dog-themed playlist!"

"Dude. I don't pirate music!" J'Shawn took the headphones off again and looked Thomas square in the eye. "I don't pirate music, I don't work for free. Making a playlist isn't that hard. You need to go."

"I can give you a flash drive. Here." Thomas fished into his pocket and pulled out a small memory stick, which he tried to hand to J'Shawn. "But I don't have —"

"G.O. Go. Go now." J'Shawn cut him off and refused to take the memory stick Thomas held out.

Thomas sighed, put the memory stick back in his pocket, and walked to the other side of the room, glancing back at J'Shawn occasionally with a scowl as he did so.

J'Shawn put his headphones back on and turned back around. Was the timing off? Boom-shak-a, boom-shak-a. Maybe it should have been shak-a-boom, shak-a-boom instead? He backed up the track, again and again, trying to own the rhythm in the sound.

He saw his shadow obscured by someone who had chosen to stand behind him. "Thomas, I already told you," he started.

And then was embarrassed to see L'Monica standing where he had expected Thomas to be.

"Sorry to bug you."

"You're not Thomas. You don't bug." J'Shawn assured. "What can I do for you?"

"Maybe nothing. I don't have fifty dollars," L'Monica admitted quietly. "But I was hoping, maybe. Ebony said you might —"

"I was just giving Thomas a hard time. Dude is constantly trying to bum stuff and never gives anything back. Ebony said you two been talking. What's on your mind?"

"Well, I've got Rosemary."

"Yeah, I like your photo montage things. They're pretty sweet. You need some music, though."

"Right. But since I don't have a lot of money, I was wondering if I could put you as my add-on."

"I'm intrigued. Tell me more."

"Well, I have a list of options people can choose from when they do a portrait session with me. I could add 'music by J'Shawn' and whatever you would charge me for that, and then come to you if someone chose that option and paid me for it."

"Hmmm." J'Shawn pretended to think it over. He didn't need to though. He knew a win-win when he heard it.

"I mean, I could try to get some money together for a sampler, maybe, but I figured most people already know your music and..."

"No, you're good. I like the idea. I think it's a win-win."

L'Monica blushed and smiled.

J'Shawn thought she had a great smile. She was so shy though. It was hard to tell what she was thinking. Not like Ebony. You knew everything with Ebony -- even if you didn't want to know.

J'Shawn realized L'Monica wasn't actually going to say anything else without being prompted. "I don't mind putting some sample music together for you. Why don't you grab the bus home with me and you can pick out some stuff you like."

L'Monica literally stepped backwards. "Sorry, my momma wouldn't like that. You can bring me whatever, it's fine. It's fine."

In her rush to get away, L'Monica nearly knocked over a desk. She grabbed up her books and was out the door a few seconds before the bell rang.

Ms. Mathis was talking to Jason and didn't appear to notice. J'Shawn thought that was good. He didn't want to be the reason L'Monica got in trouble. But what was all that about her mamma saying 'no?' Was she scared of him because of his court case? Did she think he was a thief? Who actually listened to everything their momma said, anyway?

J'Shawn picked up his backpack and headed for the door. Jason had the right idea. Getting mixed up with girls was only good for trouble.

Thomas

Why did J'Shawn have to be such a tool? No one in class had a spare fifty dollars laying around. And then L'Monica walks up and basically asks for the same thing and he tells her yes. That's not fair!

Thomas may have walked away from J'Shawn, but he didn't stop paying attention. Everyone treated him like a pariah. They would all work together, but just because he tried to add bling to some dog collars, no one would work with him.

Damn that Ebony!

It wasn't his fault. He didn't have any money to buy materials to make a product. And he really felt the service he provided was good enough he shouldn't have to make anything. He walked dogs and he shoveled their crap. What was he supposed to do -- make art out of it?

Jason had his shirts. Ebony was showing Ms. Mathis her phone cases. So bling was in.

When Thomas had swiped some of his little sister's nail accessories (thinking she would never miss them) and set about adding bling to the dog collars while he was out on walks, of course, the dog owners hated it. They didn't want extra stuff on their dogs' collars. And they were mad that Thomas didn't ask first. Of course, the one time Thomas did ask, he was told 'no.' How would the dog owners know they wouldn't like it before they could see it for themselves?

But then he got in trouble at home when he was trying to tell his mother about how awful his clients treated him. He hadn't meant to tell on himself, and his mother absolutely missed the point. No matter what he did, it was wrong. He was wrong. Well, he was tired of being wrong.

He slipped the collar out of his pocket. Mitzi the poodle had outgrown it and the owner didn't need it. So why shouldn't Thomas have it? And he was already in trouble for taking his sister's things, so why shouldn't he keep using them? He taped the collar onto a piece of paper and wrote "Bitch Bling" and "Butch Bling" at the top. And just like Ms. Mathis had told them, he created a business plan around selling the collars. Maybe he could find a puppy owner to sell the poodle's collar to. Everybody was against him, but he could still make it. Sometimes, he even felt like he was against himself, but if he just kept pushing, he knew that he was going to make it.

But he didn't make it. He was lucky he still had his job. It was hard not to get attached to the dogs. Hard not to want to take them home. Hard not to pretend like they were his. They were the only living things not looking at him like something he scooped up off the sidewalk. J'Shawn stole something and was on probation and could still tell him no and treat him like the dog crap he shoveled on the daily. Everybody in that class was helping each other in some way. Who was helping him, already?

"What's your problem, loser?"

How long had Ebony been standing in front of him? And who was she to call him a loser? Thomas had enough of being treated like dirt.

"You! You're my problem!" Then Thomas did something that even shocked himself. He hocked up a loogie and spit it right in Ebony's face. Bullseye! Then, he ran out of the classroom. Let them suspend him. He no longer cared what they did.

J'Shawn

J'Shawn stood over the counter in the Family and Consumer Science lab. Mr. Baynor called it a lab. It was still a kitchen. They made food. They didn't dissect frogs.

The quantities and ingredients swam around on the page. He took a piece of paper out of his notebook and folded the top part down. He tore out a small rectangle, then held the paper over the recipe, trying to isolate each measurement and ingredient to make it easier to read.

Some days, it wasn't so bad. Other days, like today, it was terrible. He had so much to make up from his time in court. And the time he spent worrying about what was going to happen.

He tried to shake it off. He had to focus. Cooking wasn't hard. And Mr. Baynor was really understanding about his dyslexia and the court stuff -- letting him come and make up this assignment was just one example of how he did. Other kids made up cooking assignments at home, but the stove at his house didn't work too good, and the landlord didn't want to replace it.

The worst thing was, cooking with a recipe didn't allow for a margin of error. Make a mistake on a math paper, the rest was still okay. Switch two letters on an English paper and the teacher might not even notice if the rest of the paper was legible or there was such a big stack to grade that no individual assignment got a lot of attention. However, mess up one ingredient, like sugar or flour, and the whole thing turns out wrong. Even if everything else was measured perfect, take one bite and know that all that hard work was for nothing.

Two eggs. J'Shawn got the eggs out of the fridge, set two in a bowl, and moved the paper to the next line.

A half stick of butter. J'Shawn got out a stick of butter and a knife, cut the butter stick down the middle, and put the half he wasn't going to use back in the fridge. He set the other half, still in its wrapper, in the bowl with the two eggs he hadn't cracked yet. Then he moved the paper again.

Sugar. But was it one half cup or two cups? He blinked his eyes and tried to make the numbers stay in one place. It wasn't working.

"What are you still doing here J'Shawn?"

Ebony and Shanae came in together. Ebony sat down at the four-person circle table. Shanae walked over to J'Shawn, the recipe book, and the paper.

"I'm baking a cake. What does it look like I'm doing?"

"Touchy!" Ebony said. Then she got really interested in her manicure.

"What's this paper for?" Shanae asked.

"Sometimes I get the ingredients or the amounts mixed up when I'm trying to read them. That's all. Sometimes the paper helps." J'Shawn wasn't sure how much he wanted to admit. He didn't want to admit it wasn't helping him much at the moment.

"You need my app." Shanae told him. "I made it for my little sister, but it will work for anybody."

"Isn't that your product? Aren't you selling that?" J'Shawn's budget was tight, like really tight, but he didn't blame Shanae for trying to make a sale. They were all hustling. All the time. It was the only way to make it.

"If you'll give me a five-star rating, I'll let you in as a BETA tester," Shanae said good-naturedly.

"Well, all right. If you're sure. That could be a big help."

"Wait a minute," Ebony said. "Don't download just yet."

"It's OK, Ebony," Shanae said. "Here, hand me your phone, J'Shawn."

He handed it over. She navigated to the app store.

"I said wait a minute," Ebony insisted.

"And he doesn't have to give me five stars," Shanae continued tapping on J'Shawn's phone. "He knows I'm just teasing about that."

"But I want something."

Shanae stopped tapping. She raised her eyes up from the phone to connect with Ebony's. The look was half interested, half shade. "This had better be good, Eb."

J'Shawn's shoulders slumped. Ebony did not think small when it came to getting what she wanted. "What do you need, Ebony?"

"A five-pound bag of sugar."

"Say what?" J'Shawn dropped the measuring cup.

"I need a five-pound bag of sugar." Ebony did not look up from her nails.

"What you need sugar for, much less five pounds of it?" Shanae put her hand on her hip. The other clutched J'Shawn's phone, one step away from downloading her app on it.

Ebony looked up at Shanae then, and bold as a lioness said, "I'm gonna bake my grandma a cake. OK, nosey?"

"You ain't gonna make no grandma no cake," J'Shawn said. "You don't need no five pounds of sugar to make a cake for nobody."

"Maybe my grandma really likes sugar." Ebony made her eyes all wide and innocent looking, but her friends were not buying it.

"Your grandma'd die of diabetes if she ate a cake like that." Shanae said, amused.

"Cut the crap, Ebony. What you really want five pounds of sugar for?" J'Shawn put the dropped measuring cup in the sink, wiped his hands on his apron, pulled a chair out from the table, turned it around backwards, and straddled it so his face was really close to Ebony's.

"I'm going to teach that Thomas a lesson." Ebony crossed her arms over her chest.

"Girl, are you still on about him?" Shanae asked. "Surely he'd quit ribbing you if you stopped giving him such a reaction."

"He spit in my face. IN MY FACE!"

"You called him a loser," Shanae said matter-of-factly.

"Whose side are you on?"

"I'm on yours, of course. But maybe if you just left things alone a minute," Shanae tried to reason with Ebony. Not for the first time.

Ebony wasn't having it. "That punk never leaves me alone. Steals my ideas. Insults me. Always around. You two are going to graduate in a few months. I have a whole other year with him. He has got to be put in his place!"

"So you're going to give him diabetes?" Shanae teased. "You know it don't work like that."

"Ah, Shanae, just shut it! He made me into a meme! Bling Bitch! Remember?"

"J'Shawn, help," Shanae said.

"Yeah, I remember." J'Shawn did his best. "I also remember you trying to shut his business down."

"Well, he deserved it. He was copying me."

"That's not what the judgment came down."

"Whose side are you on, anyway?" Ebony pouted.

"Ebony, you know you're my girl and I got no love for Thomas. But I don't think Thomas works you over as much as the Joker does." He hated bringing her on again, off again ex into the conversation, but some perspective was needed.

"I told you we're broke up!"

"Yeah, but for how long? And Joker doesn't get near the reaction Thomas does."

"Well, Thomas is a little punk!"

"Girl, I'm not arguing with you. But you're still mad over something a classmate pulled months ago."

"He spit in my face TODAY!"

J'Shawn ignored that, since Shanae had already addressed it. "Your friends had your back then, we led a boycott of his business, and we got the meme to go away. And your bling is still selling, right?"

"He spit in my face." Ebony said again. She looked away from her friends. Still pouting, she said, "I knew you wouldn't understand. That's why I didn't want to say anything."

"Ebony, you are still my best friend, even when you and my sister have the same maturity level. I still love ya, girl, but day-um." Shanae turned to J'Shawn. "Here, J'Shawn. You can just use the app on my phone. You don't have enough memory left on yours."

"Thanks." J'Shawn was pretty sure he didn't have enough memory to download a text message on his phone, much less an app. But he'd forgotten about that in the moment. Oh well. Just one more thing in his far-from-perfect life. "How do I use it?"

"It's pretty simple. You take a picture of the page you want read to you, and then you click this button and it reads it. Tap the screen to pause and unpause."

"What about when my hands are covered in flour?"

"Oh!" Shanae stomped her foot. "Never mind. I'll just read the dang thing to you. Sugar. Two cups."

J'Shawn listened and obediently followed Shanae's instructions.

Meanwhile, Ebony alternated between sitting at the table huffing and puffing and walking around the lab. She opened cabinets and shut them – not quite slamming, but not gentle, either.

J'Shawn knew she was still listening to him and Shanae, because he was cutting up and sometimes he would hear her laugh, too – before she realized they were listening to her and she caught herself.

When the cake was in the oven and the icing had been whipped, Shanae and Ebony left. Ebony had a weird smirk on her face. J'Shawn hoped she had settled down. But he had a bad feeling.

Jacob

Jacob was the first person to arrive in Mr. Avery's classroom after school. BRB was written in large letters on the whiteboard, so Jacob took the opportunity to explore his classroom. A large colorful poster of the periodic table was laminated and affixed to the wall across from him. Next to that, there was a poster of metric weights and measures. On the table underneath was a paper-doll figure his middle school teacher had called Gallon-Man. Gallon-Man was a robot-looking paper doll puppet whose body was a gallon, and whose legs and arms were smaller units of measure that fit inside the space of the body. Jacob walked over to the figure and pressed the arms and legs up for old time's sake.

"Careful. If you tear Gallon-Man, he will haunt your dreams," teased a female voice behind him.

"Sorry," Jacob spluttered, dropping the figure. "Sorry."

The next thing Jacob knew, a young woman with shoulder-length wavy hair and dark eyes had closed the distance between them. She was just slightly shorter than he was and she smelled like cotton candy.

"Good thing for you I'm not tearable like the paper doll. I'm Maggie. You're Jacob." It was not a question. Maggie held out her hand.

"Hi. I'm Jacob," Jacob replied in a daze. "Mr. Avery has me on the Science Bowl team."

"I know," Maggie said, dropping the offered hand. "I'm the captain."

All Jacob could think was that it was going to be a very good year in science. He hoped to be making lots of discoveries.

"Mag-gie!"

Jacob recognized the voice before the curly headed five-four teen stepped into the room.

"Oh. And you are already here," the teen said, indicating Jacob. "Hmm."

The two boys sized each other up.

"You are Jacob. I am Arnold Awazi. I am the physics genius that helps Maggie win Science Bowl." Arnold looked quite pleased with himself.

What Jacob took for the other members of the group entered shortly after. Arnold introduced them.

"This is Steven, chemistry, and Ross, earth sciences."

"They specialize so we can focus on what we're already good at," Maggie explained. "But anyone can buzz in on any question. Just don't get it wrong."

"Or it won't be pretty," Ross said. Then he snorted. Ross was all arms and legs and coke-bottle-thick glasses, which he pressed up into his face with his third finger.

"What's your claim to fame, fellow genius?" asked Steven. He was a pudgy red-head with a terrible case of acne. But he seemed friendly enough.

"Jacob is a geneticist. Or he will be," Maggie spoke for him. "And that means he'll working with me. Biology is my specialty."

"All the sciences overlap a bit, so don't think you can have Maggie all to yourself," Arnold warned.

"Be nice, gents," Maggie cautioned. "I don't belong to any of you. We work together, we win together. Right?"

Arnold and Ross gave a half-hearted grumble of agreement as Mr. Avery walked in the door.

"Hello, Mr. Avery," the team, minus Jacob, chorused in unison.

"Hello, team," Mr. Avery replied. "I see you've met our newest member."

"Yes, we were just getting acquainted with Jacob," Maggie said. "I think he'll be a fine addition to our team."

"Splendid, splendid," Mr. Avery said, somewhat distractedly. "Today, in honor of our new recruit, I thought we'd get out the buzzers and just try a round. What do you say?"

The team members each grabbed a buzzer and sat across from Mr. Avery, who was sitting on a lab table in front of the Gallon Man instead of behind his desk. He looked a lot more comfortable there then he did in the principal's office, Jacob thought.

Jacob also grabbed a buzzer and sat at the end of the table next to Maggie.

"For ten points," Mr. Avery announced, "multiply the number of legs an arachnid has by the number of ribs in the average member of the Anura order."

Anura order, Jacob thought. That was a frog. How many ribs did a frog have?

Buzz!

"Arnold."

"The product is zero," Arnold said.

"Good," said Mr. Avery. "Explain."

"Certainly. An arachnid is a spider, and so has eight legs, of course. However, a frog does not have ribs, so the number eight multiplied by a factor of zero is, of course, zero."

"Very good. Next question."

"Mr. Avery, can we take five?" Maggie asked.

"Sure. Let's take five," Mr. Avery replied.

Maggie turned to Steven, who had just burst out laughing. Ross was laughing, too.

"What's the joke, guys?"

"Frogs don't have ribs," Ross choked out between spasms of laughter.

"But until they finally croak," Steven hooted, "they rib-bit, rib-bit!"

"Croak." Maggie said dryly, but she was smiling. "Cute, men."

She turned to Jacob. "Perhaps I should warn you that some of us don't get out much. However, it is so much better to get all the giggles out during practice. A laughing fit during competition wrecks your concentration. Unless, of course, you can use one member's laughter to distract the other team."

"Isn't that a little underhanded?" Jacob asked.

"Sure," Maggie grinned. "That's what makes it fun."

A short while later, the laughter subsided. Mr. Avery got up to ask the next question.

Jacob put his hand over his buzzer like Maggie showed him.

"For ten points. Give an example of an emulsion with polar and non polar compounds."

Buzz!

"Arnold again."

"Salad dressing is an example of an emulsion with polar and nonpolar compounds."

"Explain."

"The most basic form of salad dressing is oil and vinegar. Vinegar is a polar compound and reacts only with itself. Oil is a nonpolar compound that only reacts with itself. So were one to put these two ingredients into a bottle and shake them up, the result would be shaken oil and vinegar compound, an emulsion, not a solution."

Maggie must have seen the confusion on Jacob's face. "You've made powdered drinks before, right? Lemonade or something?"

Jacob nodded.

"Good." Maggie appeared to think for a minute, but Jacob thought she was probably just pretending to think so he wouldn't feel as stupid as he was feeling. "So you put the powder and sugar into a pitcher and then you fill it with water, right?"

"Right."

"And then what?"

"Then you have to stir it."

"And if you don't stir it?"

"The powder won't dissolve."

"That's right."

"And if you leave it in the fridge, even after you stir it, sometimes particles go back to the bottom and you have to stir it again or shake it."

"Exactly. But even though you might have some residue that settles at the bottom, water and sugar are both polar. The polar solid dissolves into the polar liquid."

Steven added, "Most liquids that you think of are polar. But a few are non-polar. Oils are non-polar. Can you think of anything else?"

Jacob thought for a moment.

Ross stood behind Steven, mimicking a steering wheel.

"Gasoline?" Jacob guessed.

"Very good," Steven said.

"Ross was unfairly assisting," Arnold said condescendingly.

"No points were awarded," Ross insisted. "Jacob's new to all this."

"Besides, we get points for not going with the obvious fart jokes, right Maggie?" Steven asked.

"Steven, you get all the points for not resorting to fart jokes whenever gas is mentioned," Maggie said.

Again, Jacob noticed that her tone was dry, but her eyes twinkled. It was obvious she cared about her teammates.

"So I've got a question," Jacob ventured, hoping he sounded somewhat intelligent. "If gasoline is liquid, why do we call it gas?"

Steven and Ross looked at each other and high-fived. Arnold did not look impressed.

Jacob beamed. These were his people, after all.

"All right, team, very good," Mr. Avery said. "Next question."

Thomas

"What the hell?"

Thomas looked at the white substance that was on the ground below his gas tank and rear wheel. There were also streaks of the white sandy substance down the side of the car on either side of the gas tank.

Should he touch it? He wondered. Call the police? He looked down at his phone. The battery was dead, of course. He couldn't even take a picture for evidence.

He ran back into the building, heading to the office. Surely someone would still be there and be able to check the security cameras for him. His car was the only decent thing he had. If someone had messed it up -- he didn't want to think about it.

Halfway to the office, he heard what sounded like arguing coming from one of the hallways. It sounded like J'Shawn and someone else -- Jason, maybe? Against his better judgment, Thomas turned toward the voices. It sounded like they were coming from the consumer science kitchen. Was it just a coincidence that they were still at school when something happened to his car? If so, why were they arguing about it? He thought about ignoring them, and continuing to the office, but then he thought he heard one of them say his name. He crept closer to listen, careful not to be seen from the classroom door. He hoped nobody would notice him while he was in the hallway, but the hallways were more empty than not, and it wasn't like he had a lot of friends, anyway.

"I don't know, man," J'Shawn was saying. "Girl was just tripping. Maybe she wasn't gonna do anything to Thomas with it. Maybe she was just gonna bake her grandmother a cake."

"Dude, you're on probation. If anybody finds out -- you gotta get ahead of this."

"Don't you think I know that? But it was too late as soon as she left. I can't leave the oven on and risk the school burning down. I can't turn it off and ruin my assignment. Girl's gonna do what she's gonna do -- she'll have done it already, knowing her."

"So why did you let her?"

"Dude, have you ever successfully told Ebony NO about anything?"

There was a beat of silence.

"Exactly. And that's what I'm saying. She must have stuffed her pockets full of sugar..."

Sugar. Thomas didn't need to hear another word. Ebony put sugar in his gas tank. She got it from J'Shawn. They weren't getting away with it. Jason was an accomplice, too. All of them just trying to hold him back any way they could. Thomas raced to the office. Hopefully someone would still be there.

When Thomas got to the office, he was surprised to find L'Monica there. She looked upset.

"What's wrong, L'Monica?"

L'Monica turned to face him. "Have you been out to your car?"

"Yeah. It's why I'm here. Do you know something about it?"

"Yeah. I told Principal Bellamy just now. I'm sorry I couldn't stop her."

"Ebony."

L'Monica nodded.

"Thing is, it isn't even my car," Thomas said.

"What do you mean? You've been driving it all year."

"Yeah, well, my brother got busted for DWI and lost his license a while back. We didn't have the money for another car, so my folks agreed I could drive his while he couldn't. But when I get home, he's gonna kill me."

"Maybe it won't be that bad. Maybe someone from the autoshop class can fix it."

The principal stuck her head out the door. "Oh, good. Thomas, you're here. L'Monica -- I thought I told you to go home."

"I missed the bus and Mom's still at work. She'll be off soon, though, and then she can come get me."

"Do you not have a friend you can call?"

L'Monica looked at Principal Bellamy pointedly. She didn't have many friends and she'd just ratted out one of them.

"Right. What time is soon? For your momma to be off?"

L'Monica looked at the clock on her phone. "About fifteen minutes from now, usually."

"And she'll be able to take off and come for you?"

"It'll be alright, ma'am," L'Monica assured her.

Principal Bellamy turned to Thomas. "So I guess you already know what happened."

"Yeah. J'Shawn gave Ebony sugar to put in my gas tank."

"Thomas!" L'Monica said.

"J'Shawn?" Principal Bellamy looked confused. "L'Monica, you didn't tell me J'Shawn had anything to do with this."

"J'Shawn didn't do anything, Principal Bellamy."

"So where did the sugar come from?"

L'Monica looked at her hands and didn't say anything.

Thomas thought about changing his story. He could pretend he didn't hear Jason and J'Shawn talking. That would help L'Monica not feel uncomfortable. But then he thought about how J'Shawn had refused to help him, and then turned right around and agreed to help L'Monica instead. And he gave Principal Bellamy an earful.

Shanae

"You were supposed to get me from school, Shanae," little sister was complaining bossily. "Teacher had to call the neighbor."

Shanae closed the fridge. It would have to be macaroni and cheese again. She hoped the milk that had expired two days ago would still be OK and got out a saucepan. "I thought you were riding the bus today. Like everyday."

"Nuh-uh. Play practice." Sister clambered up to her seat at the table, which was covered in envelopes marked "past due."

"Well, I'm sorry, sis. I honestly thought you were still riding the bus."

"You're late. What were you doing?" Sister was not about to let Shanae off the hook easily.

"A friend needed my help. Making a cake."

"Ooh! Cake! Can I have some?"

"Sorry, sis. It was for school."

"You have to make cakes for school? For homework?"

"Well, I don't have to this term, but my friend did."

"Your friend. Not Ebony. So a boy. Is he your BOY friend?" Sister accused mockingly.

"He is a boy. And he is my friend. You remember J'Shawn. Don't you?"

"Music J'Shawn?"

"Music J'Shawn. That's right."

"He made the music for our play. Ms. Angela likes him."

"Is Ms. Angela still doing the after-school program?"

"Uh-huh."

"With the glasses on the chain?"

"Yup."

"And that..."

"Yup."

"I didn't even say what."

"It's not nice to say. But she does."

"Fair enough. She was the supervisor when I was in after-school. J'Shawn and I were there together when we were your age."

"Yeah. She's an old lady. But we're not supposed to say."

"That's right. Calling people old is rude."

"Are you gonna marry J'Shawn?"

"No, I don't think so," Shanae laughed.

"Then I think I'm gonna," Sister declared.

Shanae couldn't help it, she laughed harder. "Sis, you're eight years old."

"So?"

"So eight year olds don't need to be thinking about marrying no teenage boys."

"Why not?"

"Oh, sis. Come here," Shanae held out her hands, and Sister climbed up into her lap and laid her head on her older sister's shoulder. It was just as well. Shanae knew lots of reasons why little girls shouldn't make wedding plans with teenagers, but none that would make the particular eight-year-old on her lap happy to listen. Instead, she wisely changed the subject. "So what play are you doing?"

Sister started talking about the play. Her plans of marrying J'Shawn seemed to have been forgotten.

Thomas

Since the car was now part of a criminal investigation, Principal Bellamy had a police officer take Thomas home. Thomas was relieved that he didn't have to be the one to explain everything. Life in the house was hard enough.

His mom actually acted like she understood what Thomas was going through. She made his favorite food — fried pork chops with pork and beans — for dinner. Afterwards, Thomas and his little sister had ice cream for dessert. As far as rotten days went, Thomas knew his could have been a whole lot worse.

After dinner, he did his homework, showered, and then went to bed around ten. He was almost asleep when he heard his bedroom door open. He squinted his eyes closed against the thin stream of light coming from the hallway. He knew, in the back of his mind, that he should have gotten up. He should have at least tried to run or curl up in a ball, or something. He should have known that his brother was just biding his time.

"I told you not to let anything happen to my car!" Jeremy growled.

Thomas kept his eyes shut, praying that Jeremy just wanted to scare him.

The first blow of the baseball bat hit him square in the head. Luckily, the top bunk overhead made it difficult for Jeremy to aim the bat just where he wanted. If Jeremy had even been sober enough to consider that.

After a few unsuccessful blows to the shoulders, and one that made his ears ring, Thomas was dragged off the lower bunk. He kept his eyes squeezed tight. He tried to pull his blankets around his head. He passed out long before his brother finished with him.

L'Monica

L'Monica couldn't sleep that night. She tossed and turned. Ebony was going to be so mad at her. She hoped that Thomas's car would be OK. She wondered how Thomas got home. She hoped J'Shawn would be able to explain letting Ebony walk out with the sugar. She knew that was Ebony's plan. She had heard J'Shawn telling Shanae he would be in the culinary arts lab after school, and then she had heard Ebony talking to someone on the phone about getting sugar for a gas tank. But she didn't know who Ebony had been talking to.

She had really hoped she would get to Principal Bellamy before Ebony was able to go through with it. That was why she hadn't been with Ebony and Shanae when they went to see J'Shawn. But the principal had been in meetings, or something, and so L'Monica had had to wait. Someone from security had called Principal Bellamy on her cell. She had come back to find L'Monica waiting. She hadn't asked a whole lot of questions – so L'Monica hadn't had to volunteer anything. But she hadn't stopped it, either.

And why did Thomas choose yesterday, of all days, to tell her it wasn't even his car? L'Monica figured someone was not making his life easy at home. Too many times he had a black eye or an odd bruise. Usually he said one of the dogs tripped him, or two dogs were fighting and he had to break them up, got hurt in the process. But she knew he'd been lying. Should she have told Principal Bellamy that, too? But she hadn't known the car belonged to Thomas's brother. Not until the damage was already done.

She tossed and turned, and without really knowing why, finally cried herself to sleep about an hour before her alarm went off. It was going to be a long, hellish day.

***

L'Monica had been able to avoid everyone else and go directly to her morning classes. However, she knew she her luck would fail her when she got to BETA class.

She knew she had to face the music -- and the wrath of Ebony. However, when she got to Ms. Mathis' classroom, only Jason and Shanae were there. No J'Shawn, no Ebony, no Thomas. She didn't dare look directly at Jason or Shanae. They weren't directly involved, but they were still going to be mad. She walked past them to her seat and opened her book.

She expected Ebony to walk in any minute, calling her a bitch and telling her she was dead. In a way, she welcomed it. Having Ebony tell her off would lessen her guilt. And if she had the guts for it, she might tell Ebony off in return. She may have been planning to tell, but she hadn't actually told. Ebony didn't have to do anything that rose to the level of vandalism, but she actually did. And she didn't have to have involved everyone else — especially J'Shawn. In fact, the more L'Monica thought about it, the madder at Ebony she got.

She was not at all surprised when Ms. Mathis called a class meeting. She figured Principal Bellamy would have told their teacher about all the shenanigans.

"Class, I have some difficult news," Ms. Mathis began.

L'Monica waited.

"Last night, Thomas was very badly beaten. He's in the hospital in critical condition."

L'Monica gasped. She remembered just yesterday how Thomas had said his brother was going to kill him. She was horrified that he apparently hadn't been exaggerating.

"Mrs. Shepherd asked me to ask you to pray for her son. And I think that we should take a minute, but nobody has to, if it makes them feel uncomfortable, but take a minute to say a prayer or to send a thought of healing for Thomas."

Shanae

Shanae looked over at Jason and raised her eyebrows. J'Shawn and Ebony weren't in the classroom. Who knew what hell was breaking loose? Had Ebony gotten J'Shawn to beat up Thomas for her?

Should she have gotten more involved? Would it have made a difference? She thought back over the events of the past few days. She helped J'Shawn make the cake. She tried to talk Ebony down. Did Ebony go back to the culinary arts lab after they left J'Shawn to bake his cake? Shanae wasn't even going to try to hope that they weren't involved with whatever got Thomas beat up.

Still, beatdowns weren't J'Shawn's style. So what happened? Where were her friends?

Ms. Mathis released them to their work stations, but it was clear nobody was going to get much done.

"Where's J'Shawn?" Jason asked her.

"I don't know," Shanae replied. "Do you think he's mixed up in this?'

"Don't you?"

"Yeah."

"Ebony messed up his brother's car," L'Monica said.

Shanae and Jason turned around to see the shy sophomore who had just spoken up.

"What do you know about it?" Shanae said.

"Ebony was caught on camera doing something to the car's gas tank. Only Thomas has just been borrowing the car. It belongs to his brother."

"What did she do?"

"Couldn't tell. The image was grainy, and she was standing in front of whatever she did." L'Monica said. It might have even been true. L'Monica just knew that Principal Bellamy had already been told. There was no reason to admit she was going to rat out their friend. Even now.

"Well, maybe she didn't do anything, then," Shanae hoped out loud.

"If she didn't do anything, then she would be here," Jason tried to point out softly, but it still came out kind of harsh.

J'Shawn chose that moment to walk into the classroom. "You will never believe the morning I just had," he said. "And when I see Ebony again, remind me to slap her upside her fool head for all the trouble she got me into!"

J'Shawn

Ms. Mathis cleared her throat as a warning that J'Shawn could not tell the group what had happened since they saw him the day before. So they all sat and accomplished nothing until the bell rang for lunch.

"Tell us everything," Jason said.

"Leave out nothing," Shanae added.

"Are we going to the cafeteria, at least?"

"Figured if your probation was going to get taken away, you'd rather tell us in private," Jason suggested.

Now J'Shawn raised an eyebrow. "It's going to take more than an angry Ebony to keep J'Shawn Gosset down," he said. "I feel bad she and Thomas have beef, but they can leave me out of it."

"So you don't know," L'Monica said timidly.

"What don't I know?" J'Shawn said.

"Thomas is in the hospital."

"Hang on a minute," J'Shawn said. "What?"

"Someone beat Thomas up last night," Shanae said.

"We thought maybe you did it for Ebony," Jason added.

"No way. I told Ebony yesterday that I wasn't going to help her."

"But she took the sugar from you. You told me that yesterday," Jason said. He had a confused look on his face.

"Yeah, she stuffed some handfuls into her pockets. I don't think enough to hurt anything. And that's what I told Principal Bellamy this morning."

"You didn't beat anybody up?"

"No. I did not beat anybody up. Do you not know me at all? You and my grandmother."

"Your grandmother?"

"Yeah. Principal Bellamy called us into her office this morning. About the missing sugar. But she ended up saying it was no big deal and that I didn't need to worry about it. And she wanted Grandma to hear it from her and not think I was getting somebody to call for me or some shit -- I'm not sure and I don't care. But we get into Principal Bellamy's office, and before she even starts telling us why we're there,

Grandma starts like she's gonna cast some demons out of me. And she's moaning and crying out for Jesus and causing such a big racket. I wanted the ground to open up and just swallow me whole."

"Dude, was she playing?" Jason wanted to know.

"I think that's just Grandma. She's worried I'm going to be some crackhead like Momma, so she's always praying over me and stuff."

"Could you imagine if she'd gone with you to court?"

"It's a damn good thing I'm eighteen," J'Shawn agreed.

"Guys, what about Thomas?" Shanae said.

"What about him?" J'Shawn asked. "Where is he? Someone beat him up. OK. He have a black eye or something?"

"He's in the hospital." L'Monica said in a quiet voice.

"Oh." J'Shawn said, stunned. "Oh! That's not good. He trying to join a gang or something?"

"He came to the office yesterday after Ebony messed with his car," L'Monica said. "He told me that his brother would kill him if anything happened to that car. I guess he tried."

"But nothing's wrong with the car. It was in the parking lot this morning. It looked fine," Jason said, getting up to indicate they were all going to the cafeteria after all.

"But she wasn't planning to do anything to the body of the car. She was going to mess up the gas tank," Shanae said.

"Principal Bellamy wasn't sure it was safe for Thomas to drive the car home, so someone gave him a ride," L'Monica said.

"You know a lot about it," Shanae said.

L'Monica didn't answer.

"What will sugar do to the gas tank?" J'Shawn asked. "I know she was talking about it yesterday, but I wasn't really paying attention to her plan -- just how she was trying to involve me."

"I'm not one hundred percent positive," Shanae admitted. "But I bet I know who does know."

"That guy who helped you with your app?" Jason asked.

"Or one of his friends, yeah," Shanae replied.

"Well, let's go talk to them."

They got up from the table.

L'Monica mouthed, "thank you" to J'Shawn.

J'Shawn smiled. "I got your back, girl."

"What did you say?" Shanae asked.

"I said 'lead the way,'" J'Shawn said. Then he turned to L'Monica and grinned.

Jacob

Jacob watched the group walk toward them. One girl in front led the way confidently. The others ambled behind her, looking slightly guilty and nervous. Perhaps they should. People usually only approached the nerds' table when they wanted something.

"Hey guys," the lead girl said. "I have a question for you."

"Is your app working successfully Shanae?" the physics guy asked. "Or is there any malfunction?"

"The app is working great, Arnold. You're a lifesaver."

Jacob noticed Arnold blush a little. He was a little surprised he could see it.

"My question is unrelated to my app," the girl, Shanae, continued.

"How can we help?" Steven asked -- a little too eagerly, Jacob thought.

"What would sugar do to a gas tank?"

Now it was Jacob's turn to blush. He had missed that question yesterday. He would not miss it again. "Nothing. Or at least, very little."

"Explain, please," Maggie requested after exchanging some microscopic look with Shanae.

"Well, people used to think if you put sugar in the gas tank, you would mess up an engine," Jacob explained. "But anyone who has made lemonade knows that sugar dissolves in water very easily."

Shanae thought for a minute. "That does make sense," she said finally. "But why didn't all the adults know that? There's a kid in the hospital right now because..." Shanae trailed off for a minute.

"Not because something happened to the car," Arnold said. "He was assaulted. Correct?"

"Yeah. You could say that," Shanae said.

"I did say it," Arnold said. "Assault is what happened to Thomas."

Jacob had no idea how the Science Bowl people even knew Thomas, whoever that was, or anyone from the group in front of him. Wasn't Shanae and the guy with her seniors? He thought maybe the girl in the back of the group might be in a class with him, but he'd never heard her speak, and wasn't sure if she even could.

He looked over at Maggie. She had that same deep-in-thought look he noticed she had when she was listening to Science Bowl questions. Did she know any of these people? Were they friends of hers?

"Well," Maggie said finally, "Arnold would be the one to know. He keeps a finger on the pulse of things."

"How do you do that?" the other boy in the group, Jacob couldn't remember if anyone had said his name, asked. He had headphones around his neck where most athletes would have a post-shower towel. The effect was similar.

"I, uhm, have my ways," Arnold said mysteriously.

"Yeah, one of those ways is a police scanner he built himself," Steven interjected.

Maggie, Arnold, and Ross gave Steven a hard look.

"You don't need to be volunteering that information, Steven," Maggie said. "Civilian scanners aren't technically perfectly legal to have."

"Correction Maggie," Arnold said. "My device is perfectly legal. I simply cannot use it while driving or to commit or aid in committing another crime. Still, certain people in authority do not take kindly to their authority being thwarted by shared information. I try to respect authority in these matters."

"I guess you do," said the head-phoned teen. "So, do you know if Thomas is going to be alright? And who hit him? Or do you know what happened to Ebony?"

Shanae put her arm up to stop the flood of questions from the head-phoned boy.

"I suspect Thomas will be released today or tomorrow. They were most concerned about head injuries, but this time, he was lucky." Arnold stopped to poke some salad with his fork. He put a green forkful in his mouth, chewed slowly, then swallowed. Jacob thought he was enjoying the attention.

"So who did it?" asked the head-phoned guy impatiently.

"She knows. Don't you, L'Monica?" Arnold indicated the quiet girl.

L'Monica. That was her name, Jacob thought. And probably they had math class together. That was a class you never had to talk in unless you had a question. If her grades were good, she wouldn't ever have to say anything. Jacob suspected her grades were good.

"He said his brother would kill him if anything happened to the car," L'Monica said quietly.

Jacob noticed that she had a camera around her neck. The camera was odd because most people just used their phones to snap pictures. Maybe she was on newspaper or yearbook or something like that.

"A slight exaggeration, potentially bordering on hyperbole, but perhaps he thought he was in danger."

Arnold's bluntness was not unkind, but Jacob thought he sounded kind of arrogant. He looked to see the expressions on Maggie and Shanae's faces. But if Arnold's lack of politeness bothered them, they didn't show it.

"So where's the brother now?" Headphones wanted to know.

"Booked and released last night."

"So Thomas is going to go back home and his brother's still going to be there?" L'Monica asked. The horror in her voice replaced the shyness.

"Like over ninety percent of abused children in the United States," Arnold replied. "Though abuse by siblings is not always figured into the statistical data. Some would say Thomas was bullied, not abused. Others would seek to know his mother's involvement or the length of time of the abuse, whether or not physical harm was escalating, and so forth, before making a determination."

"He's going home where his brother is," L'Monica said again. Color drained from her face as if the weight of that fact was pressing the color out of her.

Shanae pulled L'Monica in for a hug, and then kept her there, in the crook of her arm. Headphones and the other boy looked around awkwardly.

The whole group was quiet for a minute, each left to their own thoughts in a quiet bubble surrounded by the noise of the rest of the students in the cafeteria.

Headphones broke the silent bubble. "Was the brother just looking for a reason?"

"Probably." Arnold said. "He already has a criminal record and a drinking problem. And the father is out of the picture. Those things make a situation ripe for gratuitous violence."

Gratuitous violence? Was this guy for real? Jacob wondered. But again he looked at the girls, and again he saw no trace of annoyance at the message tone or delivery. Just sadness. One more high schooler becoming little more than a statistic on the scatter plot of life.

Shanae

As they left the cafeteria, Shanae fished into L'Monica's jacket pocket and pulled out her phone. She found the contact "Mom" and pressed "call."

When it went straight to voicemail, Shanae hung up without leaving a message. "Plan B," she said.

She put L'Monica's phone back in her pocket and guided the sophomore to the counseling center. "May we have a room, please?" she asked the student who was stationed there. The student pushed a sign-in notebook at her and Shanae signed them both in. "Can you let her fifth period teacher know she's in here? And sixth, if we're still talking?"

"You can only do peer counseling for one academic period. After that, you have to have a staff member with you or go back to class," the student said, as if reciting something she said many times a day.

"That's fine," said Shanae. "We'll work with what we've got. Thank you so much."

She ushered L'Monica into the empty room, turned on the lights, and shut the door. The couch looked like something drug up from a basement back in 1970. Threadbare plaid cushions sat on top of a wooden frame. Dog eared pillows sat at each armrest. It was unlikely that they had cushioned anything comfortably in quite some time.

"Well, it's better than a classroom, and an excused absence from class," Shanae said brightly.

L'Monica looked at her gratefully, but she didn't smile or speak.

"I was at your grandmother's funeral, you know."

L'Monica looked surprised.

"Sure. Ms. Rosemary volunteered reading to the kids at the library summer program. Thomas, Jason and I all took our sisters. Well, Thomas dropped Ruby off and walked dogs, but Rosemary didn't mind that. And Jason dropped his sister off with me. She and Sissie are buddies. Well, I guess they all are, but Thomas's sister Ruby never came home with Sissie." Shanae realized she was running on and stopped herself. "I didn't mind. It's easier to watch two of them entertaining themselves than to be expected to entertain one who doesn't have her friend." Shanae thought for a minute. "You don't have brothers or sisters, do you?"

"No, it's only me. I've always wanted siblings, but..."

"Well, you can't judge every relationship by Thomas and his brother. Though lots of siblings argue and fight, sometimes even roughhouse with each other, it doesn't usually end in someone being hospitalized."

"I thought siblings were supposed to look out for each other."

"They often do. But sometimes..." Shanae wished the room had a window. It felt very cramped. She started again. "Look. Sissie and I fight from time to time. But she's my sister and I love her and I will always protect her. Thomas and his brother, I guess they aren't like that. In some families, it's hard to see the love for the abuse."

"But if Thomas was being abused, why didn't he tell someone? Or protect himself better, at least?"

"It's kind of like tornadoes. They can brew up any time, so you kind of get tired of watching for them, because you can't wrap yourself or your house in bubble wrap and still live. But whether or not you protect yourself, you are getting destroyed. The storm comes too fast for help to help you, even if it wants to."

"How do you know about it?"

"Sissie's dad was a real jerk to my mom. Mom put up with it for a while, because it was easier to live in the house with two paychecks coming in. But one day he got mad and hit me. Mom wasn't going to have that. I guess that makes me one of the lucky ones."

"What about your dad?"

"What about him? I never knew him. Isn't yours gone, too?"

"No. Military. He's in the Middle East somewhere."

"Oh." Shanae looked at L'Monica again. "Oh. I just assumed..."

"Everybody does. I'm used to it," L'Monica said. "So many families don't have a dad in the picture at all. And mine has been deployed for most of my life, so it feels like it's just Mom and me, but I know Dad's doing what he needs to."

"So was he at Ms. Rosemary's funeral?"

"No. He wanted to be. But Mom said she could handle it."

"What about you? Can you handle it?"

"I think it's like Mom says. We do what we have to. And we can't save everybody."

"Your Momma is smart."

"We can't save everybody," L'Monica mused again. Then she sat up straighter. "We can't save everybody. But can we help somehow?"

"Help? Like how?"

"I don't know... Take up a collection for his medical bills or something? Help fix his BETA plan, maybe? He needs something that's HIS, but I'm not sure he's going to get there on his own."

"You may be right about that. Let me talk to Jason and J'Shawn. And find out where Ebony is, too. Ms. Mathis may also have some ideas -- and maybe after his hospital stay, Thomas will be more likely to listen."

L'Monica giggled. "I wouldn't count on it."

Ebony

Ebony's unplanned, unscheduled campus tour of the state college was just the thing she had been needing to lift her spirits. When the Delta Gamma sorority sister arrived at her door yesterday, Ebony did not question her good fortune. Juniors and seniors in good academic standing were allowed up to five days a year for campus visits. Ebony hadn't used any of hers. But with her big sis for the day, she toured campus, attended a political science lecture with a handsome TA, ate lunch in the food court, and even managed a decent serve in an impromptu volleyball game that had started in front of the DG house.

She had practically forgotten about Thomas the next morning. Principal Bellamy's instructions had said to come to her office the day after her campus visit before going to classes, so that was what Ebony did.

Ebony did not expect what she found there. Sitting in the hallway outside the principal's office was an almost unrecognizable Thomas. He had a black eye and the whole side of his face was an ugly shade of purple. Part of his hair had been shaved, revealing a line of stitches that started a handwidth from his forehead and ran across the back of his skull to a place about even with his earlobe. One arm was cast and in a sling. The other was covered by an oversized jacket.

Ebony remembered when she wore her jacket three sizes too big like that. Her arm underneath was scratched and bruised, and she didn't want anyone to touch it or see. She pushed that thought out of her mind.

Memory pushed aside, she asked, "Did your dogs finally turn on you, Thomas?"

"Hey, Ebony. Yeah, something like that."

Principal Bellamy stuck her head out of her office. "Oh, good. Ebony, you're here. I'll be with you in just a minute. Thomas, child services wants to know if you want to file charges."

"Charges? What charges?" Ebony asked.

"We'll talk in a minute, Ebony. Thomas?"

"I'm not filing charges."

"Are you sure?"

Ebony saw the saddest smile she had ever seen on Principal Bellamy's face as she heard Thomas say, "I'm sure."

A long silence hung in the air.

"Can I go back to class, Principal Bellamy?"

"Sure, Thomas. Do you need help?"

"No, ma'am. I got it."

Ebony watched Thomas struggle to his feet. She almost forgot she was mad at him as she forced herself not to help him stand up. She understood pride. This person was not the same one who had spit in her face two days ago.

She backed up against the wall to make sure he had plenty of room to get around her.

"OK, Ms. Ebony." Principal Bellamy said. "Join me in my office whenever you are ready. I want to hear all about your college visit."

Ebony continued to press herself against the wall as she watched Thomas try to figure out the best way to pick his backpack up off the floor. It was hard to watch, but Ebony could not force her eyes away. Thomas used his non-slinged hand to grab the top loop of the back. Ebony could tell he wanted to sling it over his shoulder, but there must have been an injury there as well. Finally, he raised the backpack to his waist, stuck his thumb in his front belt loop, and used his leg to push the weight of the backpack in front of him. Slowly, he made his way to the door of the hallway. The backpacked hand pushed down on the handle of the door and he pulled it toward him enough to get his foot in the space. Then he shuffled through the doorway and was gone.

Principal Bellamy was on the phone when Ebony walked into her office. She took a seat at the desk, despite all the piles of folders. Ebony knew that the conference table was like the special parlor room that old people used to entertain company. In Principal Bellamy's house, Ebony was not company.

"What happened to Thomas was not your fault," the principal covered the phone receiver with her hand while speaking to Ebony. Then she covered her other ear as if to hear what the caller was saying.

"My fault? Why would it be my fault?" Ebony asked.

The principal didn't appear to be listening to her. She swiveled her office chair around to face away from Ebony, her fingers twirled around the cord of the office phone.

"Why would what happened to Thomas be my fault?" Ebony asked again, voice rising.

Principal Bellamy held up a finger from the hand that was not wrapped in the phone cord, indicating "wait."

Ebony sat back, seething. What did Bellamy mean, it wasn't her fault? Of course it wasn't her fault. She sprinkled some stuff around his gas tank. She didn't call out a hit on him. She was just trying to scare him a little. It certainly wasn't her fault if he pissed off somebody else who decided to rough him up.

But what did Bellamy know that Ebony didn't know?

"Thanks. You, too. Have a great day. So, Ebony, tell me about your college visit," Principal Bellamy said as she hung up the phone.

No. Ebony was not playing. "What happened to Thomas?"

"I really can't discuss other students with you."

"What happened to Thomas? Tell me!" Ebony gripped the arms of the padded stationary chair, as if letting go would launch her across the files and into the principal's face.

"What happened to Thomas was not your fault and I don't want you blaming yourself." Principal Bellamy answered with the practiced ease of a professional who was not baited by another person's anger or excitement.

"What is not my fault?" Ebony changed her question, hoping to get a different response.

"It is not your fault that when a strange white substance was found around Thomas' gas tank, and the police decided the car was unfit to drive until testing could be completed, which took several hours, and so Thomas went home without the car, which was actually his brother's, so the brother thought the car was badly damaged, which it wasn't, and decided to punish Thomas, which is why the ADA is considering pressing charges. Thomas won't actually get a say in that, but knowing whether or not he would be willing to testify as to what happened would make the ADA's case easier. You remember last year."

Ebony remembered last year. She remembered looking at Principal Bellamy through one black eye and one very blurry slit where her other eye should have been. It wasn't her fault, then, either, but she still hurt and she still had to be the one to cover the worst of the bruises with makeup. People think black girls don't bruise visibly, especially when they are dark-complected, and the makeup didn't do anything to help her open her eye. It did give her shaking hands something to focus on. Yes, she remembered last year.

And just like then, she refused to ease the silence with her own words. She and the principal stared at each other across a desk covered and piled high in files.

"Good," Principal Bellamy began, "because I could see how a sensitive individual such as yourself might blame yourself for what happened. And I don't want you doing that." She smiled that same heartbreaking smile again -- the smile that said she was a witness, not a savior. The smile that said she loved her students enough to let them make whatever foolish decisions they were going to, and then support them as they picked up the pieces by themselves afterward. It was the smile that said she wasn't accepting responsibility for the things that happened outside the walls of her school, even if she had feelings about it.

"So why did you call me in here really, Bellamy?" she dropped the principal's title, trying to put them on equal footing.

"I wanted to make sure my soror did her job showing you around campus, letting you get a feel of things. A lay of the land, if you will."

Soror. Sorority sister when the sorority was predominantly black. Ebony knew this now. It was something she had a chance at, now.

"Why yesterday?" she asked.

"It did occur to me," Principal Bellamy said, "that if my classmate was in the hospital and we had been pushing back on each other, I might feel some guilt about harm that came to him. And it did occur to me that you don't need that kind of guilt in your life."

"But yesterday I didn't even know."

"I know. And if I had my way, you wouldn't know today. But that's not how the world works. I'm not about to keep you out of school and from your education. And yesterday, you needed to see a piece of the world that is waiting for you."

"I know I have things going for me. I have Bling Thing and I have Nationals and I'm almost a senior."

"You don't have Nationals, Ebony."

"Say what?"

"I'm going to Ms. Mathis's classroom to make the announcement in person, but at the budget meeting, they cut the funding I was going to use to send you to Nationals. I can send two, and so I'll send Jason and Shanae, and hopefully I'll send you next year."

"But that isn't"

"Fair?" Principal Bellamy cut Ebony off. "Girl, you know that life isn't fair. You know that bad things happen to good people and you know we fight uphill both ways every day and that's just how it is."

Ebony sat back in her chair, deflated like a balloon.

Principal Bellamy stood and walked around her desk to take the seat next to Ebony's. "I thought you might not react well to the announcement. Your class has been hit with a few things pretty hard, and I wanted to space them out if I couldn't change them. But I lost my last appeal two nights ago."

Ebony stared dully at her principal.

"If you had known about Thomas, or the budget, you would not have been able to enjoy your campus experience. I wanted to at least be able to give you that."

A fat tear formed in the corner of Ebony's eye. When she tried to blink it away, it rolled down her cheek instead. She tried to catch it with the knuckle of her pointer finger, but instead just pushed it into the crease between her nose and the corner of her mouth. Unbidden, more tears followed the path.

Principal Bellamy did not reach out a hand or even hand Ebony a tissue, Ebony realized. She sat there, close enough to touch, but not touching, until Ebony grabbed a tissue for herself and caught the tears that insisted on making their way down her face, one after the other after the other. Not because she was heartless, but because she understood.

L'Monica

Underneath the stairwell was a space big enough to be a popular semi-private makeout spot for one lucky couple, which changed throughout the course of the day. But today, all couples felt no love as Jason's body blocked the entire entryway. Shanae, J'Shawn, and L'Monica found themselves cramped inside.

"We've all seen people who've been messed up before," Shanae was saying. "What we can't do is go in there and fall apart all over him. It's just another day."

"What we can't do," J'Shawn was arguing, "is let Ebony run rough over L'Monica and try to pin responsibility on her. Did you call her last night, Sha?"

"I didn't. Sissie wasn't feeling well and Mom was working, so Sissie had curled up into me watching a movie and I couldn't get to my phone without moving her." Shanae adjusted her weight to the other foot. "And I didn't know what to say, anyway."

L'Monica thought about all the advice J'Shawn had given her for Ebony's return. Don't back down. Look her in the eye. Don't raise your hands or get backed into a wall. Shanae had advice, too. Make fists at waist level or keep hands on hips. Don't raise your voice. L'Monica didn't know why there were so many rules about engaging Ebony.

The bell rang then and they had to hustle to get into the classroom. Just as they were about to pass through the doorway, they saw Ebony walking with her head held high and her books to her chest. Right behind her was Principal Bellamy.

"Now what?" J'Shawn heaved in frustration.

Ms. Mathis looked at the stragglers coming in her doorway. Thomas had taken a seat near the back, clearly trying to position the freshly shaved part of his head in the corner of the room where it was least noticeable.

Ebony came in and put her books on a desk in the front row but did not sit. Principal Bellamy came in behind her.

"Ms. Mathis, I apologize for my intrusion. May I address the class?"

Ms. Mathis was about to say yes when Ebony decided she was going to rip off the Band-Aid. "Look people. Principal Bellamy's come here to tell us that them dudes in admin done cut her budget again, so we can't all go to Nationals." She paused for just a minute to let this sink in, but not long enough for either Ms. Mathis or Principal Bellamy to take control. "Right. And you know I love you, Jason and Shanae, because you're the seniors and you're the ones picked to go, even though Jason, you've already been and won the thing TWICE," she paused just long enough for Jason to wince, "everyone is going to drop everything they thought they were doing this weekend so we can raise the money for the rest of us to go and because some of us have bills to pay."

L'Monica thought Ebony was looking over everyone else's head in such a way she was either looking at Thomas or a very interesting poster on the wall.

"And just to clear the air," Ebony said. "The feud with Thomas is over. There are so many adults ready to count us out. We can't waste time hating on each other. So now we need to put our heads together and try to figure out what we are going to do this weekend to raise the money we need. Principal Bellamy? Ms. Mathis? How much money is that?"

L'Monica watched the teacher and the principal putting their heads together behind the teacher's desk.

"Ebony," Jason began. "I love this change and this new you we are seeing, but this weekend is no good for me. I've had the photoshoot scheduled for weeks."

L'Monica knew that wasn't exactly true, but no one corrected Jason. He'd had to reschedule to fit the photographer's schedule. This was the last weekend possible before the competition. It was now or never for him. And as a senior, it was his last chance.

Ebony looked everywhere but at him. L'Monica understood why. Ebony knew about Jason's photoshoot, of course. She was even supposed to model in it. But Jason being out -- and getting to go to Nationals regardless -- that was a tough pill to swallow. L'Monica thought he should have kept his mouth shut. But at the same time, that would have been a lie, too. If only things didn't seem so bent on keeping them down!! How were they going to make it?

"I can't go to Nationals anyway on account of my probation," J'Shawn said. "But you just tell me what you need. I'm there for you."

Ebony shot him a grateful look.

"We still need an idea," Shanae said. "Can we afford the ingredients for a bake sale or something?"

Everyone looked around uncomfortably.

"Probably not the best thing for me," J'Shawn said.

"And people probably don't want me near sugar anytime soon," Ebony said. She tried to laugh.

Everyone else groaned.

"Point taken! It was just an idea," Shanae said, raising her hands defensively from her seat. "Who has a better one?"

They looked to the adults in the room first. The adults didn't look back right away.

Finally, Ms. Mathis said, "Every student in this room has established a business they had planned to present at Nationals. How can those businesses help you achieve your current goal?"

Shanae and Ebony looked at each other. Shanae's app hadn't been market tested. She was planning the official launch at Nationals. Ebony was the opposite. She'd been selling at school whenever she could and on Saturday mornings at the Farmer's Market. Market saturation, Ms. Mathis called it. Until the next smartphone upgrade came out, people weren't going to be buying more phone cases.

Before she knew what was happening, all eyes were on L'Monica.

"Could you sell photos of people maybe?" Shanae asked gently.

"Yeah, maybe," L'Monica replied. But inside her head, she was thinking about the cost of printing photo packages, getting a printer on site. She normally took a few hours per shoot. Even putting in a full day on Saturday might only mean five clients. What she really needed was a way to take a bunch of pictures for a bunch of clients in less time, and still make something they all wanted.

"Well, that wasn't the enthusiasm I was hoping for, but it's a start," Ebony said. Let's keep thinking about how we can get people to come let L'Monica take their picture and pay us the big bucks. OK?"

"Sounds good," Shanae said. "And I'll talk to Arnold and the Science Bowl people again at lunch. Maybe they'll have some insights."

Thomas

True to their word(s), the members of the BETA team focused on ways to make money so more people could go to the competition. The way Thomas saw it, though, L'Monica and Ebony were the only two non-seniors that were even eligible to go. There wasn't going to be any money for anything else, if there was even enough money to add the two of them.

He looked over at J'Shawn, who nodded in his direction. He hadn't realized J'Shawn's bogus probation prevented him from taking the trip. Nationals were in Atlanta, not on the moon. But J'Shawn didn't need BETA competition. He would play football on scholarship in the fall.

"Thomas, come sit with us," J'Shawn called.

"I'm alright," Thomas said. Ebony said the feud was over, but that didn't mean he wanted to sit by her and risk starting it again.

"Thomas, we are brainstorming, get over here!" Ebony commanded. But Thomas recognized that there was no heat in her words now. Of course, she wanted to go to Nationals, and the only thing she needed was money. Thomas saw himself as a means to an end with her. But he guessed that was preferable to being hated. He got up slowly and made his way over to the BETA table.

"Where do Shanae and L'Monica usually sit?" Thomas asked.

"Oh, sit anywhere," J'Shawn said. "They are going to be at Maggie's table. Could be there all lunch period."

Thomas carefully sat at the table.

"Tell me your number. I'll get you a tray," Ebony said.

"I'll just," Thomas began.

"Number!"

"Eight six nine two."

"Got it. Be right back," Ebony said.

Jason was huddled over his phone. Whatever he was doing or reading, he wasn't liking. "Excuse me," he said, and got up from the table, dialing numbers as he walked away.

When it was just the two of them at the table, J'Shawn asked, "Who'd you get to walk your dogs for you?"

"Ruby did yesterday, for the few clients that still wanted somebody. Mom drove beside her the whole way. Most of the owners said they would handle it themselves until I got better. I'm hoping I'll be less stiff tomorrow. Walking the dogs again will help."

"Well, don't be afraid to call me. We can get some people together to walk with you or help."

"OK. Thank you. Leashes can get tangled when I've got two good hands. An extra pair or two wouldn't hurt right now. I think I will take you up on that," Thomas said.

"What will you do?" Maggie said, coming to their table. "Shanae and L'Monica have invaded my table, so I've come to bug you guys. You don't mind, do you?"

"Not at all," J'Shawn said.

"Go ahead," Ebony agreed, she set a tray down in front of Thomas. "Here you go."

"What did I interrupt?" Maggie asked again as she sat where Ebony indicated.

"J'Shawn offered to help me with dog walking while I am figuring things out," Thomas said.

"Ooh! I love dogs! My mom is allergic, so we can't have any in the house. But I'd love to help! And I bet Steven and Ross would, too. I'll ask them."

"Do Steven and Ross like dogs?"

"I don't know. But they like me. Where I go, they go."

"Well, that's confidence," Ebony laughed. "What are they talking about over there?"

"Photography. Shanae thinks L'Monica can set up a photo booth at the Farmer's Market. But L'Monica seems reluctant about it."

"L'Monica's shy," Thomas said.

"I know. I've met her before. But this is different than that. Arnold's talking to her about other things they can do with apps or something. Hey -- what about pet photography?" Just like that, Maggie jumped up. "Hey team, gather round!"

The Science Bowl team left their usual table to stand around Maggie. Shanae and L'Monica followed.

When they were all around Maggie, she said, "you are talking about doing a photoshoot this weekend, right?"

There was a chorus of "yeahs," but L'Monica wasn't saying anything.

"And you need to make money for your trip without spending a lot on materials."

L'Monica perked up. "Go on," she said.

"So what if Arnold created a photo database for area pets? Science Bowl could collect the information from the owners, and L'Monica could take pictures of the pets. Owners, too, but charge extra for that. People would pay five to ten bucks for their pets to be included in the database, and then if they wanted prints of their session, they could pay L'Monica extra for that and she could print the pictures at home. After they pre-paid."

Everyone looked at L'Monica expectantly. Her worried expression slowly changed into a smile. "I think that could work," she said.

J'Shawn

"You're on probation. You're not a flight risk. Why did you think you couldn't go to Nationals?"

"Judge?" J'Shawn recognized the woman who had presided over his first and last court appearance, but then he realized he didn't know her name. She had two dogs, Rottweilers, on leashes. "What are you doing here?"

"Here" was next to the dumpsters outside the Farmer's Market. The pet photography business had a great turn-out that morning, and lots of people donated to help pay Thomas's medical bills, too. Business was great for everyone. Ebony was getting orders for adding pictures of people's dogs to custom phone covers. L'Monica was getting all sorts of appointments for future photo shoots. Jason's photographer bailed last minute, so Jason gave L'Monica the balance and she took pictures of him and his models when there were no other customers in line. Sometimes the models helped hold the dogs if their owners didn't want to be in the pictures. L'Monica promised to take more pictures for Jason on Monday if he didn't get anything he could use. Shanae had a group of kids trying out her reading app when there were no dogs to pet or cuddle. The Science Bowl members had been true to their word, both helping Thomas walk the dogs that week and collecting dog owner's information for the dog lover's database this morning. There was plenty money for all the BETAs to go to Nationals. Feeling left out once again, J'Shawn had come behind the dumpster to vent his frustration out of earshot from his classmates.

"Ben, sit. Jerry, sit. J'Shawn, did you hear my question?"

"Yes, your honor."

"Then answer me. Why did you think you couldn't go to Nationals?"

"I don't know. I just thought I couldn't."

"But you kept working on your Nationals project. You could have goofed off. You could have coasted. Your grades were good enough. You already have a scholarship to play ball. So what were you doing staying after school and baking cakes and doing this music stuff for a competition you thought you weren't able to compete in?"

"Football is my ticket into college, Judge. I work hard, but it isn't enough. My test scores weren't that great. My grades are good enough for honor roll, but only because I work really hard at it. I need a degree in business, and football is my ticket. If I am really lucky, I could go pro in a year or two. The right endorsements, and I might never have to work again. But a sack goes wrong before I have my other ducks lined up? I'm out. My chances are gone." J'Shawn wanted to kick the dumpster again, but he didn't want to startle the Rottweilers. So he held his hands down at his sides and tried to keep still and non-threatening.

"The entertainment business is a hard one," the judge said. Loops on the leashes were around her wrist. She gathered the line and held it in her hand.

"Entertainment business, Judge?"

"People buy tickets to watch boys knock each other senseless in unscripted fashion. It's entertainment, I suppose. But then there are people who create art and poetry and music. Some of them make it. Some of them are paid really well. But whether football or music, it's hard work."

"I've never been afraid of hard work."

"Mmmmm," she murmured in agreement.

They stood there together, not saying anything. At the ends of the judge's leashes, Ben and Jerry moved from their seated positions to laying on their backs, legs in the air, sunning themselves. Jerry's back legs pawed the sky.

"Do me a favor." The judge almost made it sound like a question. "Actually, two favors."

"Do you need music to walk your dogs to?" J'Shawn asked.

The judge chuckled. "I think we are set. I downloaded your music to work out by app a few weeks ago. Normally I prefer music with lyrics, but it was nice."

J'Shawn grinned at the compliment. When people loved his music – well, there was nothing in the world like it. He looked at the judge. "So what's the favor?"

"I know you think a lot of people have counted you out. I won't even say you're wrong about that, because I don't think you are. You are a young black man and life is tough for young black men. Even the athletes, actors, and music stars."

"Look, I don't mean any disrespect," J'Shawn said.

"Don't interrupt me," said the judge.

"Yes, ma'am. I'm sorry, ma'am," J'Shawn apologized quickly.

"But while you are keeping it real like that — while you are there knowing just how hard it is and how many people are looking to count you out — don't get in your own way. There's a difference between being determined and being impulsive. And there's a difference between relying on people like a scrub and demanding that the system work for you."

"Yes, ma'am."

"Did you ever file a complaint with the Better Business Bureau over the headphones?"

"No."

"Well, some people trusted the system and filed complaints of their own, though I imagine one or two complained on your behalf and weren't actual customers."

"They did?"

"They did. I looked into it, like I said I would."

J'Shawn didn't know what to say.

"Have you been to the mall recently?"

"Grandma asked me to stay away."

"And none of your classmates told you that the store was gone."

"What?"

"I had made a few calls, and a case was being built around the store owner. The DA tells me a fraud case was filed. It was filed the same afternoon of the day you were in my courtroom. Had it been a day earlier, I would have been able to dismiss all the charges."

"Really?"

"Really. But it didn't happen that way. Anyway, when they went to serve the store owner with the notice of action, the store was empty. Security cameras show she had cleared everything out the night before, skipping her last month's rent and making herself look very, very guilty in the eyes of the law."

"But that's it, then? She leaves town, sets up shop somewhere else, and gets away with it?"

"What goes around comes around. You may not see it, but I do think you can trust it. Which brings me to my other favor," the judge said.

J'Shawn noticed she didn't disagree with him. But she didn't agree with him, either. It still wasn't fair. "So get out of my own way. And then... Then what's the other favor?" He asked.

"When you are making that list of everyone counting you out, I don't want to be on it. I'm going to keep tabs on the store owner situation. And I know you don't trust me yet, but I am hoping I can change that."

"Ma'am, you don't have to," J'Shawn started.

"There you go again. Favor number one. You better believe I mean it, and I'm going to bust you over it any time you break it. Get out of your own way. Trust people who try to help you."

"Yes, ma'am."

"Now it so happens that I need a trustworthy person with a reliable vehicle to run errands for me after school and this summer. We'll see how it goes after that. Will you accept the position?"

J'Shawn could not believe his ears. "Me? Come work for you?"

"I know it isn't a cushy mall job, but I think I'm a fair employer. And everyone could use some help now and then, am I right?"

"Yes, ma'am."

"So you will accept?"

"Yes, ma'am. When would I start?"

"Right away. The ladies in the office outside my courtroom tell me that people coming to see me would be less jittery with a music track playing outside. So maybe you could start there."

"I could do that. Yes, I could do that."

"And next, I have another promising young man who owes me some community service. He's very creative, and I think he might have some new ideas to help you with your reading. I'll expect you to be honest with me if he does not take his community service to you seriously. Do you understand?"

"I think I do," J'Shawn said.

"Good. Finally, your first delivery. I don't normally carry these with me, but I was rather determined, in this particular incidence, that you would accept the job and save me a trip." The judge handed J'Shawn two envelopes.

J'Shawn furrowed his eyebrows and gave her a questioning look. "These are both addressed to me."

"Then I hope my new courier can get them to their intended recipient without delay." The judge smiled. "Go ahead, open them."

"Alright." J'Shawn opened the first envelope. It was a legal finding of not guilty due to lack of evidence. A full acquittal. He looked at her to confirm. "Am I reading this right?"

"No more probation," the judge confirmed. "Despite your admission of guilt, the court found a distinct lack of evidence, and you are free to go, as you always should have been."

J'Shawn was stunned.

"Now, I realize I made you that job offer before you had this in your hand. That may not have been fair of me. If you would rather work at the mall or a restaurant or something, I would understand. I just didn't want you accepting a position I offered out of misplaced gratitude. You are a fine young man capable of earning a position on your own merits."

J'Shawn could only nod and shake his head, not trusting his voice.

The nodding and shaking may have confused the judge, who asked, "Do you still want to work for me?"

J'Shawn nodded, swallowing hard. "Yes," he barely managed.

"Good. Now open the other one. This is fun." With the loops of the dog leashes securely around her wrist, she dropped the lines she was holding and clapped her hands giddily, like an excited child in front of a stack of birthday gifts. The dogs didn't seem to notice or care.

J'Shawn opened the second envelope. Inside were his BETA Nationals registration confirmation, some gas station gift cards, and a room reservation. All paid for.

"No refunds and no exchanges, do you hear me? You go to Nationals and you kick butt next weekend," the judge said. "I'm counting on you."

"You got it," J'Shawn choked. "You got it."

L'Monica

L'Monica zipped up her bag while Shanae waited. A lot had happened in the past week. Each BETA's contributions toward the doggie database had put spending money in their pockets and given them a new confidence with which to approach Nationals. And now they were all going.

J'Shawn and his grandmother were driving Thomas and Jason. Shanae was riding in Ms. Mathis's car with L'Monica and Ebony. Everyone was in high spirits.

"You got everything?" Shanae asked.

"I think so."

"Your flyers? Tablecloth? Candy?"

"Check. Check. Check."

"Clean underwear?"

"Yes, mother," L'Monica groaned good-naturedly.

Outside, the horn honked.

"Guess we better get going," Shanae said. She and L'Monica had been hanging out together a lot. L'Monica enjoyed getting to know Shanae's little sister. Sissie enjoyed L'Monica's being shy, because she could talk all she wanted and L'Monica didn't seem to mind.

"Can you believe how quickly things change?" Shanae was saying. "Two weeks ago, I was trying on my cap and gown and thinking about all the people who counted me out.

L'Monica just nodded. It had been a roller coaster the past few days -- and now it felt like they were on top, looking over the whole city.

The hour-long drive to Atlanta was over in a blink. Ms. Mathis surprised them by parking at the Ponce City Market. The market was well known for having an amusement park on the roof.

J'Shawn pulled in next to Ms. Mathis and everyone got out of the cars.

"Why are we here?" Shanae asked.

"Didn't you know?" Ms. Mathis said. "Nationals is vending at Ponce City Market this year. And, as one of Jason's perks for winning last year, we got the chance to secure accommodations here instead of a hotel."

"Did the judge know that?" J'Shawn wondered. He still couldn't believe everything that the judge had given him for this trip.

"Yes, she worked with me to make sure we were all going to stay in the same place. There's even a small room for your grandmother and me to share so you teens don't feel stifled."

J'Shawn's grandmother looked at Ms. Mathis gratefully.

As they walked through the already crowded market, they saw other schools setting up their tables and displays in the walkways beside the well-established venues that were permanent parts of Park City Market. They saw the sign for East End right next to the food court entry.

"Great placement!" Ms. Mathis said. "You are going to have so much foot traffic. You won't have a dull moment."

They dropped their bags off in their rooms, ate dinner, and then Ms. Mathis took them to the glass elevator that led to the amusement park on the roof.

"Closed for private event," J'Shawn read. "Figures."

"Oh, but we ARE the private event," Ms. Mathis said. "Besides. I know the rules the judge gave you. You just broke rule number one. Stop it."

J'Shawn ducked his head. The judge would be busting him a lot over that one. Old habits are hard to break.

Jason looked at J'Shawn, "Hey man," he said. "They counted us out, but we still made it."

They exited the elevator and had the time of their lives.

About the Author

Willie Craddick Jr. works hard, plays hard, and is determined to get the most out of life. He is the author of this book and *The Life of a Boy with Big Dreams*.

He graduated high school in December and has also been taking college classes, intending to walk with his class in May holding a college associate degree!

Willie also has his own clothing business called "BASHED"- shopbashed.com. Willie isn't your average teenager; his work ethic is unbelievable!

Acknowledgments

Here are some photos from Willie's photoshoot. Unlike Jason's photographer in the story, Willie's photographer came through and did an amazing job for his client. Two of them, one group photo and one individual photo, were included on the front and back cover of this book.

And while there are many people who may have counted Willie out for one reason or another, there are also many people in his life that Willie is really thankful for. If he started naming names, someone might get left out. But his friends don't need to be named. They know who they are. And any hater who wants to be like that – they know who they are, too. None of that changes who Willie is or how he's going to make it in his life!!

Thank you for buying this book and being a positive part of Willie's dream for his future!!

91094411R00095

Made in the USA
Columbia, SC
14 March 2018